STD A

ROSEMARY COTTAGE

The discovery that an empty bakery was attached to the country cottage Holly had inherited unexpectedly, with a work force eager to start it up again, caused inevitable complications; not the least in her relationship with her fiancé.

PAT LACEY

ROSEMARY COTTAGE

Complete and Unabridged

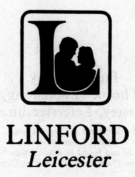

LINFORD
Leicester

First published in Great Britain in 1981 by
Robert Hale Limited
London

First Linford Edition
published December 1990
by arrangement with Robert Hale Ltd., London

British Library CIP Data

Lacey, Pat
    Rosemary cottage.— Large print ed.—
Linford romance library
I. Title
823.914[F]

    ISBN 0–7089–6930–5

Published by
F. A. Thorpe (Publishing) Ltd.
Anstey, Leicestershire
Set by Words & Graphics Ltd.
Anstey, Leicestershire
Printed and bound in Great Britain by
T. J. Press (Padstow) Ltd., Padstow, Cornwall

1

HOLLY SANDFORD leaned on the iron gate at the end of the mossy path, and gazed back at Rosemary Cottage with considerably more enthusiasm than she'd felt when Mr. Boucher had first told her of it. Mr. Boucher, as Great-aunt Gertrude's London solicitor, had been the person to inform her, only two days previously, that Rosemary Cottage, 'lock, stock and bakery', as he'd put it, now belonged to her.

Holly, with no first-hand memories of Great-aunt Gertrude, had been rendered speechless for at least half a minute. Born on the eve of her Great-aunt's departure for New Zealand, she'd apparently caused the old lady to postpone her passage in order to act as her godmother, although she hadn't returned to England since. And now, suddenly, came news of her

1

death and of Holly's inheritance of the cottage where, apparently, Great-aunt Gertrude had lived as a child. That it had a bakery attached to it had seemed, at first, quite irrelevant.

"It doesn't have to be put into operation unless you so desire," Mr. Boucher had pointed out.

"I should think not!" Holly had shaken her head with its bell of long, fair hair and scoffed at the very idea. A personal assistant to a fashion editor didn't want to be bothered with running a bakery! Nor was she at all sure that she wanted to be bothered with Rosemary Cottage either. "I'm wondering," she'd told Mr. Boucher, "if it wouldn't be as well to sell both the cottage and the bakery, without even going to look at them."

But Mr. Boucher had been shocked at the suggestion. "My dear Miss Sandford, it might be exactly what you want. Marlingham, after all, is within easy travelling distance of London."

His remark had, so to speak, stopped Holly in her tracks. Mr. Boucher's point

2

of view was one that might also be shared by Brian. Indeed, Rosemary Cottage might even be the deciding factor in fixing their wedding-day. They'd talked about it often enough, but always there had been some compelling reason — like his business trips to the States or the Far East — to postpone it.

"Go and look at the cottage," Mr. Boucher had advised. "October can be a delightful month in the country. But don't expect too much. Remember, it hasn't been lived in for six months or more."

At first, she'd hoped Brian would drive down with her, but an important client of the advertising agency for which he worked had suddenly demanded a Saturday morning meeting, and she'd come down alone. But at least she'd been able to take her time exploring every nook and cranny of Rosemary Cottage. And these, she now had good reason to know, were considerable. She'd tripped over more steps and knocked her head on more beams than she would have thought possible in such a small cottage! Even so, considering it now, from the safety of its garden gate, she felt a certain pride and affection.

It lay snugly against a tall hedge of golden beech. The thatch above the tiny dormer windows, in reality threadbare and ragged, looked smooth and thick in the gathering dusk. Across the herring-bone patterns of the old red bricks, the weathered beams rose like the branches of some ancient, silver tree.

Her eyes followed the dipping line of the thatch until it tumbled to the lower elevation of the bakery roof. In her ignorance, she'd imagined a sort of gigantic kitchen range, black and ugly. In fact, there had been only two small iron doors let into a wall, one opening into a chamber the size of a small room, and the other into an even larger area, but with its tiled floor beginning at waist-level.

Outside the bakery, with its door that opened in two parts, like a stable-door, she could still make out the outline of the old pump, its stone basin now cracked and matted with toad-flax, although the pipe had gushed a miraculous stream of pure crystal when she'd pumped the rusty, iron handle.

Frowning slightly, she turned and walked to her car. Enchanting though Rosemary Cottage could undoubtedly be made, would Brian see it in that light? The modern conveniences of twentieth-century living were very necessary to his life-style.

Two minutes later, she drove from the quiet peace of Bun Lane into Marlingham's cobbled market square. The place was a natural, pedestrians' paradise, with the trunks of tall lime trees preventing the parking of cars in front of the many shops. Holly examined these with interest; some, bow-fronted and bottle-glassed; some, porticoed and elegant in the Georgian style; others approached by flights of steps with handrails of wrought iron. Above, where stars now glistened in a frosty sky, was the infinite variety of their roofs; red-tiled and gabled, slate-grey and steep, or balconied beneath overhanging eaves.

The perfect Christmas card, thought Holly, and followed a sign to a car-park set behind a bank that looked more like a private house than a place of business.

Walking back to the square, she came face to face with an establishment that seemed to offer a variety of services under one ancient roof. Steps rose to it, and on one side of the porticoed door — hospitably ajar to show the graceful curve of a shallow staircase — a large window held a display of books; beyond, she could see tall reading-desks, wide enough for the spread of the newspapers and magazines they held. Beyond that again, an inner room was set out with tables and chairs where tea was being served by a young red-haired girl wearing a long sprigged gown and bibbed apron of delicate white lace. Over the outer door, in Gothic lettering, was the inscription 'John Lorimer. Books'. Teas must be a more modern addition.

Holly's professional eye admired the neat smocking on the girl's gown and the sensible elbow-length cuffs that kept the sleeves' fullness out of harm's way.

"Why not come inside?" suggested a deep voice behind her.

Startled, she turned to find that a man was already mounting the steps and pushing wide the door. "It's a cold evening, and at least we can offer you a cup of tea."

"Thank you very much," said Holly, following him into the book-lined room and glancing curiously around. To her embarrassment the interest was two way. Without exception, the people gathered around the desks had ceased their reading and were inspecting her closely.

For the first time that day she wondered at the suitability of her ensemble. The black tweed knickerbockers above the black knee-socks, the scarlet waistcoat over the cream woollen shirt, had all seemed appropriately rural by London standards, but now, noticing the sensible skirts and suède jackets that most of the women were wearing she wasn't so sure.

"This way," said her guide, ushering her into the room beyond. Shining copper winked in the flames of a wood fire, and Holly saw that the tables had twisted, barley-sugar legs beneath the buttercup yellow cloths. The girl in the sprigged gown came forward, smiling.

"Tea and cakes, please, Abigail," said the man. "We like," he explained to Holly, "to make our visitors feel at home."

"And do you have many?"

"We're not on the tourist route, if that's what you mean, but we do attract a certain specialist clientele. I have a small, antiquarian side to my book shop, and Abigail's cakes, of course, are known and eaten all over the county."

"I can believe that," said Holly, biting into a richly crumbling piece of the shortbread that the girl had now set before her.

"And you?" enquired her host, perching himself upon the leather-covered fender. "Are you here by accident, or design?"

Holly scrutinised the lean, scholarly face with its dark eyes and gentle smile, and noticed the strands of silver in the thick black hair. "As a matter of fact," she heard herself confide, "I may be living here before long. At Rosemary Cottage, in Bun Lane."

"That is good news" he said with great enthusiasm. "Rosemary Cottage has been waiting for a new owner for far too long. So has Marlingham itself, of course. Dreadful to think that children may grow up without ever having tasted a Marlingham Bun!"

"I — I beg your pardon?"

"Let's see. Abigail could take several dozen a day. Maybe more." So engrossed was he in rapid, mental calculations, Holly's complete lack of understanding passed without notice.

"What," she asked at last, "is a Marlingham Bun? And the name, by the way, is Sandford. Holly Sandford."

"John Lorimer. How do you do?" He extended a hand absent-mindedly. "You mean, your solicitor hasn't told you about

9

the recipe? Surely it was a condition of the sale?"

Holly began to feel a close affinity with Alice on her journey through the Looking Glass. But John Lorimer now seemed to be appreciating her bewilderment.

"Miss Sandford," he explained, "bread has been baked in the bakehouse attached to your cottage for the last two hundred years, if not longer. And the recipe for Marlingham Buns — closely guarded, I may say — goes with the deeds, so that it's automatically passed on to any new owner."

"But surely," protested Holly faintly, "there's no obligation to use the bakehouse? Especially since the cottage was a legacy to me."

"It's certainly not legally binding, if — that's what you mean. And, morally speaking," John Lorimer considered her thoughtfully, "it's a moot point whether someone who receives the property as a gift is under any obligation at all. It's not the same thing as deliberately acquiring it. Do I take it," his eye passed swiftly over the slim figure and fashionable clothes, while his mouth quirked with amusement, "you haven't the slightest ambition to become a master baker?"

"Believe me, I wouldn't even know what to do with a packet of bread-mix, let alone bake a proper loaf."

"Oh, that wouldn't be necessary. All the experts are still living in Marlingham. Ready to heat up the oven at a moment's notice, I would think. There's Bill Baxter, the best baker for miles around, and his wife, Amy. Her meringues were like angels' wings!"

Abigail, passing by at that moment with a tray of used crockery, smiled at Holly. "He's quite right. And they tasted as good as they looked."

"It's not only the cakes and bread," John continued decisively, "I like things to be *used*. I can't bear anything to lie idle, be it brains, brawn or machinery."

"I know what you mean," said Holly sympathetically. "But I really don't think I could undertake a venture of that sort."

"Sell the bakery, then, and keep the cottage for yourself," John Lorimer suggested.

Holly had a sudden vision of delivery-vans in Bun Lane, breaking the early morning peace with the roar of their engines. "I don't think I'd like to live next door to a bakery, any more than own one," she said apologetically.

"Nothing like it for cutting down on your heating bills!" he pointed out sensibly.

Holly rose to her feet. This man was being far too persuasive. "It's time I was going," she said firmly. "Please thank your wife for the delicious tea."

"Coming down next weekend?" he asked.

"Possibly." He had no right to try and pin her down like this!

"Well, spare a thought for the bakery." In spite of her protests, he insisted upon escorting her across the square and staying with her until she'd started her car.

"Would it be an impertinence to

ask for your telephone number?" he enquired. "I could tell Abigail liked you and she's rather starved of female companionship down here."

"I liked her, too," said Holly warmly. "Very much." And, without hesitation, wrote down her number on the note-pad she always kept in the glovebox of the car. Giving it to a man's wife, after all, was vastly different from giving it to the man himself.

"Thank you." Carefully, John Lorimer pocketed the slip of paper. "Well, safe journey!" He stood back a little but then, as the car began to move, leaned forward and said through the open window. "By the way, Abigail's not my wife, you know. She's my niece. Her mother is my sister Caroline." With a grin of pure wickedness, he raised his hand and stood well clear as she accelerated into the square.

Really, the audacity of him! But she knew that she wasn't really annoyed, and it wasn't likely that he would telephone her anyway. Her thoughts turned to

13

what she would tell Brian when she saw him next morning. Ridiculous of John Lorimer to suggest she might sell the bakery or start it up again. They'd find some other use for it — like a double garage and a workshop, perhaps.

Next morning, she was up early, for her visit to Marlingham had meant the neglect of her weekend chores. It was while she was trying to subdue the ambitious tendrils of an ornamental ivy, threatening to overrun the bathroom, that she began to wonder if growing plants in a garden, instead of in pots, could be a new and rewarding experience. Her father, a soldier in the regular army and now retired abroad, had never stayed in one place long enough to put down roots of any description; and her mother, Holly now remembered, had often yearned for a garden of her own. As she manoeuvred the tendrils of the ivy, she recalled that Rosemary Cottage stood on a fair-sized plot of land. Besides flowers and shrubs, there should be room for a few fruit trees. And somewhere, with a name like that, there must be a herb garden of sorts. It was ridiculous, of course, to imagine Brian in old jeans and sweater, digging a vegetable patch out of that rough tussocky grass, but it was a picture that stayed with her while she continued her work. So much so, that when she eventually opened the door to him, smooth and suave in pale, beautifully pressed slacks and matching fawn pullover, she felt a slight sense of shock; that she immediately thought of John Lorimer in his worn cords and thick, Guernsey sweater was even more absurd.

"Sweetheart!" Brian put his hands on her shoulders and kissed her lingeringly upon the mouth. She felt the familiar thrill of pleasure at his touch.

Then, holding her at arm's length, he scrutinised her carefully. "No hayseeds in the hair and straws between the teeth?"

She laughed. "Idiot! It wasn't like that at all! And Rosemary Cottage was really

15

very charming. I suppose," she looked up at him hopefully, "you wouldn't consider driving down there this afternoon?"

"Can't, I'm afraid, my darling. And nor can you. Both of us are bidden to Colin and Tessa's for supper."

"But they might like to come, too." Although, given the choice, she would much prefer to show Rosemary Cottage to Brian on her own, Colin and Tessa were old friends.

"Shouldn't think so, for a moment," Brian said dismissively.

He was wrong, however. "New car's going like a dream!" Colin enthused when Brian rang to check what time they were expected. "Can't wait to show it to you!" His voice was loud enough for Holly to hear as she stood beside Brian.

"Ask him if he'd like to take us for a drive, then," she hissed. "Marlingham's only about fifty miles up the motorway."

Apparently Colin was possessed of acute hearing. "Love to!" he bawled. "Pick you up about two."

"Well, at least it's a fine day!" said

16

Brian philosophically.

But by the time Colin's new car turned into Bun Lane a fine drizzle was falling. Holly's explanation of why it was called Bun Lane went unheeded, and the cottage, she had to admit, was reminiscent of a bedraggled old lady wearing a tattered and very faded shawl.

"Darling, I really don't think . . . "Brian began, but left the sentence unfinished, as if defeated by the utter unsuitability of Rosemary Cottage as a dwelling-place.

"Let me show you the inside." Holly found she was feeling ridiculously possessive. "It's dry as a bone, even though it hasn't been lived in for several months."

Tessa gave a dramatic shudder. "My shoes will be ruined in that mud." Bun Lane had, in fact, turned into an oozing quagmire.

"No problem there!" said her husband cheerfully. "I'll carry you. How about it, Brian?"

But Brian was too occupied in scowling

at the cottage to hear. The dormer windows under their dripping eaves seemed to scowl, even more fiercely, back.

However, Colin, carrying a giggling Tessa over his shoulder as if she were a sack of flour, was already staggering through the mud.

Like Holly on the previous day, Brian fell an easy victim to the vagaries of rural architecture; twice he nearly tumbled down the twisting, old staircase, and three times cracked his head upon the exposed beams. But, unlike Holly, it wasn't so much his body, as his pride that was injured.

"Dry as a bone, did you say?" he enquired sarcastically, gazing at an ominously dark patch on one of the kitchen walls.

"Leaking overflow," said a cheerful voice from the doorway. "Nothing you can't put right with a yard or two of new pipe."

Smiling broadly, John Lorimer came into the room. "Excuse me," he said to

Holly, "for barging in like this, but I saw the car. There's this chap I know, with some wood going spare. Wondered if you could use a sack or two?"

"I doubt," said Brian icily, "if we'll be needing to light any fires."

"You could be right at that." John's gaze travelled meaningfully over Brian's immaculate figure. "As I was telling Miss Sandford only yesterday, once the oven's alight the whole place will be warm as toast."

"Oven?" Brian turned to Holly. "You didn't mention any oven." If he'd caught her concealing the presence of a poltergeist or a resident witch, he couldn't have looked more accusing.

"Bread oven," said John Lorimer briefly before Holly could open her mouth. "I'm hoping Miss Sandford will see her way to starting it up again."

"The hell you do!" said Brian angrily. "And who are you to hope any such thing? The baker, I suppose!"

Regretfully, John Lorimer shook his head. "Nothing so useful I'm afraid.

Words are my province."

"And ill-chosen at that!" said Brian hotly.

"Brian Redfern — John Lorimer," Holly managed a belated introduction. "Brian's in advertising, so words are his province, too," she added appeasingly.

"Clever words," John Lorimer observed placidly. "Specially chosen to hoodwink the gullible among us. I'm afraid I haven't that skill, either." He turned back to Holly. "Shall I collect a couple of bags of wood, then? Just in case you decide to stay?"

Holly took the easy way out. "Thank you!" she said.

"My pleasure! Well, be seeing you soon, I hope." And with a cheerful grin he turned and left.

"Man's an insufferable idiot," growled Brian. "Where on earth did you pick him up, Holly?"

She explained about their meeting in the square. "He really was most kind."

"I can imagine! Personally, I wouldn't trust him an inch."

"If you're talking about that exciting looking man we've just seen walking down the lane," said Tessa, coming into the kitchen with Colin, "I think he's dreamy!"

"A novelty," Brian told her. "These rustics are all the same. A couple of hours in his company, and you'd be bored to tears."

"Were *you* bored to tears, sweetie?" Tessa asked Holly, slyly.

"I can't say that I was," Holly admitted.

"Get him away from his own environment and you soon would be," Brian assured her.

Somehow, Holly doubted it.

Soon afterwards they left Rosemary Cottage and, although little was said, Holly knew that the visit had not been a success. Brian would never consider living there, especially with John Lorimer so near at hand.

Although it was late when he eventually drove her home that night, he asked if he might come in for a while. Once inside, he accepted the drink she offered and

21

took up his customary position on the hearth-rug. "I've been thinking, Holly. Why don't we fix a date for getting married?"

Her finger trembled so violently on the plunger of the soda syphon she was operating the glass overflowed on to the table. "Are you serious, Brian?"

He gazed at her reprovingly. "Of course I'm serious. Surely you know how I feel about you?"

"I'd begun to think you weren't the marrying kind."

"Well, only to the right girl, naturally!"

Her face alight with happiness, she went to stand beside him. "And there was I thinking what a fiasco the day had been!"

He put his arm around her. "If you mean our visit to Marlingham, then you're right. I never want to see the place again. But some people," he assured her, "would give a small fortune to own a place like Rosemary Cottage. All those oak beams and the twisting staircase and the inglenooks. Even that deplorable old bakery. They all give it character. And it's within easy commuting distance from London." It could have been Mr. Boucher speaking! "One way or another, it should fetch a very nice sum. Especially if we put it into the hands of the right estate agent; like a chap I know called Geoffrey Crisp."

"You mean sell Rosemary Cottage and buy something else?"

"And live happily ever after! Why not?"

Why not, indeed! A mud hut or an igloo would be heaven, with Brian there to share it. She stood on tiptoe and kissed him on the cheek.

"So that's what you'll do then? Sell the cottage and that damn-fool bakery?"

It was ridiculous to feel a sudden pang of regret. And not only at the thought of selling Rosemary Cottage. She saw John Lorimer's now familiar figure, hands thrust deep into the pockets of his old, tweed jacket, shoulders hunched slightly forward; and Abigail, slim and beautiful in her sprigged gown. It would be sad not to see them again.

"You won't mind, surely?" Brian was gazing at her curiously.

"Of course not!" she made herself say firmly. "If you give me the address, I'll put it in the agent's hands tomorrow."

"Good girl!" He gave her a long, lingering kiss that set her pulses racing. Soon, she thought happily, they would be married; and then Rosemary Cottage would be no more than a memory.

2

MONDAY was always a busy day at Holly's office. It wasn't until evening, going home on the tube, that she remembered about putting Rosemary Cottage on the market. But one day more, she decided wearily, would make no difference.

In fact, it made quite a difference. That evening, while she was washing up her supper dishes, the telephone rang.

"Forgive me," said John Lorimer, "for disturbing your working week. But I just wanted to tell you I've managed six sacks of wood. All neatly piled in your very own woodshed!"

"That is kind of you!" Difficult, in the face of such thoughtfulness, to tell him that she wouldn't, after all, be needing it.

"And — about the weekend. You can't possibly sleep at Rosemary Cottage. No bed! And, anyway, it's far too cold, until the bakery's functioning again."

"What about all that wood, then?" she teased, although in a moment she would have to explain that she'd never contemplated staying for the weekend anyway.

"I suppose I could light a fire in your inglenook," he said thoughtfully.

"But how would you get in?"

"Well, actually, I've noticed there's a loose catch on one of the back windows! I must mend it for you, sometime. However, I must admit there's another reason for my ringing. To warn you there'll be a deputation."

"A *what?*"

"Deputation. Bill Baxter and his wife, old Albert Higgins and young Buckie Willis. They're all people who worked at the bakery until six months ago, and they'd like nothing better than to start it up again."

"Did you suggest they came to see me?" Holly demanded, taken aback by this unexpected development.

"Honestly, not guilty! Although I have been thinking about it practically non-stop. Maybe my thoughts got tuned into theirs."

It was now or never. If other people were becoming involved the situation must be made clear.

"They'll have a wasted journey," she warned. "I'm thinking of selling the cottage *and* the bakery."

There was a pause, pregnant even over a telephone wire. Then, "You can't do that!" said John Lorimer urgently.

"Why not?"

"Well . . ." he hesitated. "Lots of reasons. Look, don't do anything impetuous. Come down for the weekend. Stay with us. You haven't met my sister Caroline, but she'd love to have you. Abigail always does a superb shepherd's pie on Saturdays. Unless you'd rather boil an egg in your inglenook, of course!"

In spite of her misgivings, Holly laughed. "Thank you! I'd much prefer Abigail's shepherd's pie." She thought quickly. Surely Brian would understand that she must, at least, meet this deputation and explain to them in person that she was selling the cottage and the bakery. It *was* their business, after all. Which — apart from all that wood — was more than could be said of John Lorimer.

"Please tell the deputation that I'll expect them around three. But not to be hopeful!"

"Thank you very much," said John Lorimer gratefully. "Well, goodnight. Sleep well!"

And surprisingly, she did.

They came up Bun Lane in line astern; a tall rosy-cheeked man and a slim, dark-haired woman; a very old man in mole-coloured corduroys and a long, lanky boy wearing patched jeans and a black leather jacket.

Holly threw an armful of logs on to the fire she'd found burning in the inglenook, then went to hold open the front door. "You're my first visitors! Please come in!"

The convoy shuffled slowly inside,

and the leader Mr. Baxter, it must be cleared his throat. "Mr. Lorimer told us we mustn't be too hopeful, miss. He thinks you may have made up your mind already about the bakery. But before you make it final, it seemed only fair to tell you we've got all the equipment safe and sound."

"Equipment?" Other than a few tons of coal, she hadn't envisaged any equipment.

But Mr. Baxter seemed hardly to have noticed the interruption. "When old Mrs. Moss died, miss, no-one seemed rightly to know what was going to happen to the bakery. And then the next thing we heard, the old lady who owned it had died, too. In Australia. So we decided to take everything into safe keeping."

"Mrs. Baxter and I had the big stuff, the mixers and the dividers and the like. Old Albert here had the tins and peels, and young Buckie took the kettle and the teapot and the scuffling-pole. It seemed only right to hold on to everything for the new owner." He paused and smiled shyly at Holly. "We didn't know it would be a young lady, of course."

She thought that she had never seen such transparent honesty in a man's face before. And his sense of responsibility in storing equipment against rust and deterioration was praise-worthy indeed.

"All we wanted you to know, miss," Old Albert was having his say now, "is that if you did happen to open up the bakehouse, we'd be happy to serve under you, same as we did for Mrs. Moss."

"A really happy family, we were," Mrs. Baxter assured her. "Bill and Albert looked after the bread. I did the cakes and fancy stuff, and young Buckie helped me, besides driving the van and other odd jobs."

"Van? Did you take care of that, too?"

"We couldn't keep it," Bill Baxter explained sadly, "because of the log-book and the insurance. But I've been thinking. I know where there's an old horse, still lively enough, and a covered cart going cheap. Feed up the horse and paint the cart and they'd be a beautiful pair."

He stopped, and they all gazed wistfully at Holly. She gulped. It was going to be very difficult to tell these people that she intended selling Rosemary Cottage and the bakery. Recollections of the row she'd had with Brian, earlier in the week, when he'd heard it was not yet on the market, still rankled. So much so she hadn't dared tell him she was meeting the bakery staff at the weekend. Fortunately an advertising campaign was keeping him in Scotland until Sunday night.

"I take it," she said now, "that you've all managed to find other employment during the last six months?"

Mr. Baxter scratched his head. "In a manner of speaking, yes. I'm gardening for the vicar, the wife's cleaning the doctor's surgery, and old Albert's gone back to his bodging. That's chair-making, miss, if you didn't happen to know. And young Buckie's driving a bus. But we'd give it all up in a wink if we could get back here."

For the first time Buckie opened his mouth. "Why don't we show you around, miss? Explain things to you."

There were murmurs of agreement. "All right," said Holly weakly.

She wasn't to forget the pleasure they obviously felt at being in *their* bakery once again. Old Albert, reunited with his old tea-cup — the size of a shaving mug! — was moved almost to tears.

"Eh, the pretty dear! Waiting for me like that!" Carefully he stood on tiptoe to put the china pot on to a high shelf out of harm's way.

Naturally Mr. Baxter was the spokesman. "This is where we light the fire, miss — and that's the oven next to it." He showed her the little room with the tiled, waist-high floor.

"Yes, I'd worked that out," Holly admitted. "I suppose the fire has to be kept well stocked while the bread's baking?" She hoped it was an intelligent surmise.

Clearly it wasn't. Four heads turned as one, and four pairs of eyes fixed her with surprised stares.

Then Mr. Baxter cleared his throat

and spoke slowly and patiently, as to a child. "The fire's good as out by the time we put the dough in, miss."

Holly leaned against the wall, ignoring the smears of whitewash that immediately came off on to her navy, denim suit. "Suppose you tell me the whole process from the beginning," she suggested.

"Well, we light the fire in here." Mr. Baxter opened the door of the smaller chamber.

"Round about five o'clock in the morning," added old Albert.

Holly winced.

"Not on Sunday mornings," put in Mrs. Baxter quickly. "We don't bake on Sundays."

"The heat from the fire," continued her husband, "hots up the oven." As if producing a rabbit from a hat, he threw open the oven door.

"How does it get there, exactly?" Holly peered doubtfully inside.

"Through the blower," said Mr. Baxter succinctly. "If you look you'll see a hole cut in the bricks. By the time the fire's no more than embers, the oven's just right for the dough."

"Some of which we mix the night before," explained old Albert, "to let it rise."

"By hand?" asked Holly.

The question seemed to please him. He nodded. "Some of us," he looked at Mr. Baxter with a kind of fiendish relish, "use new-fangled machines. Others depend on the strength God gave them."

"There's no denying," said Mr. Baxter, "that Albert has a good hand with the dough. Punches it a fair treat. But with my other responsibilities, I find it quicker to use the electric mixer first thing in the morning. As you do," he reminded Albert severely, "if the rheumatics have got you!"

"Folks can tell the difference, though," Albert pointed out proudly.

Young Buckie suddenly cleared his throat. "Reckon you'll be wondering what I do, miss. Besides make the tea."

"Yes, what do you do, Buckie?"

"Thought you'd never ask, miss." He

grinned impishly. "Well, I do the scuffling before the bread's put in."

"Scuffling?" Holly echoed. Hadn't someone earlier mentioned a scuffling-pole?

Buckie grinned again. "When the bricks of the oven are white-hot, Mr. Baxter knows it's time to put in the bread. But there's quite a bit of ash and stuff got into the oven by then, through the blower. So I tie a piece of clean sacking on to a long pole, dip it in a bucket of water and scuffle it all out. That's scuffling, miss."

"I see," said Holly. "And what else do you do?"

"Well, beside the van, I help Mrs. Baxter with the fancy side — the buns and the meringues and the gingerbread men. That sort of thing. She makes them and I do the decorations."

"Ah, yes, the buns!" Holly turned to Mrs. Baxter. "There's a special recipe for those, I understand?"

"So I believe, miss, on a piece of old paper somewhere. But there's no need to look for it. It's clear as anything in my head. I had it straight from old Mrs. Moss who made them before me, and she had it from the lady before that. Anytime you want it, miss, I'll tell it to you."

"I must say I'd love to taste one," said Holly unthinkingly. And then, noticing the gleam of hope in Mrs. Baxter's eyes, looked hastily away. What could she ask now, to postpone the moment when they would stand and wait, patient and hopeful, for her verdict? The old iron pump caught her eye. "I don't suppose you use that now?"

"That we do!" Albert told her. "Special properties that water has, to make Marlingham bread something to be proud of. That, and the punching," he added quickly.

"It has to be the special pump-water in the buns, too," said Mrs. Baxter.

"And what," asked Holly, suddenly noticing the long tube of some sort of material that seemed to be coming out of a corner of the ceiling, "is that?"

"Flour chute," said Mr. Baxter. He

indicated a flight of stone steps that ran up the side of an inside wall, presumably into a small loft. "We store the sacks of flour up there. Then, when we want some, we nip up and tip it down the chute. Best quality linen, that is."

"Probably do with a good clean by now, though," observed Mrs. Baxter.

"Well," said Holly, for she could see nothing else to enquire about, "it's been most interesting. Thank you all very much for coming."

As she had expected, there was a pause, broken by Mrs. Baxter suddenly addressing her husband. "It's a big decision for the young lady to take, Bill. And she's not experienced in our ways."

For several minutes now Holly had known she wasn't going to have the courage to tell them, face to face, of her intentions. She would just have to explain in a letter, as tactfully worded as she could make it. Meanwhile, she smiled at Mrs. Baxter gratefully.

"You're right! There's a lot to be considered. But I promise you I'll let you know as soon as I possibly can. And I'm most grateful to you all for explaining everything to me so clearly."

And with that they seemed content. As they filed out of the bakery Holly saw a tall figure was standing outside the cottage.

"Well," John Lorimer called cheerfully, "know all about it now?"

"I'm a lot wiser," Holly assured him.

Together, they stood and watched the deputation reform and move away down the lane. "Lovely people!" said Holly.

"Any decisions reached?"

"I don't think," Holly began slowly, and then paused. When she spoke again it was as if someone else was putting the words into her mouth. "I don't think I could go on living with myself if *they* were to be let down."

"That's marvellous news!" said John Lorimer.

Holly tried to pull herself together. "I said — if they were to be let down," she said defensively. "Not if *I* were to let them down."

"Now you're splitting hairs," he objected. "You wouldn't be on your own you know."

"I wouldn't?"

"I've been doing some thinking as well. As I see it, it's in Marlingham's interest to start the bakery up again. Its closure has been severely felt I can assure you. So why don't we form a sort of syndicate, made up of townsfolk who are willing to put a little capital into the venture? I would, for one."

"Would you, really?"

"Of course! Our doctor would, too, I'm sure. He's always moaning about not getting his wholemeal bread every day!"

"Oh, we make wholemeal bread, do we?" said Holly without thinking.

"Yes, we *do!*" John Lorimer suddenly gave her a quick spontaneous hug. "*And* currant bread! *And* rye! *And* lardy cake!"

"You amaze me!" But still more amazed was she at her pleased reaction to his embrace. Clearly, his chief concern was to have a thriving bakery in the town once again, and to re-employ the old staff, but even so, working with him could be quite an experience!

3

JOHN LORIMER'S widowed sister, Caroline Forbes, had his dark eyes and gentle smile. Holly warmed to her on sight.

"It's so nice to meet someone new," Caroline told her. "I'm always telling Abbie she should widen her experience."

"I like Marlingham!" Abbie protested. "Although I wouldn't mind a new routine. If you did open the bakery," she told Holly, "I'd love to help. And I'm quite useful with a paint-brush when you come to do up the cottage."

"Not so fast!" Holly pleaded. "I haven't made up my mind what I shall do, yet." But it was almost as if they hadn't heard — or didn't want to.

After Abigail's excellent shepherd's pie had been followed by apple pie and cream, coffee was taken in the parlour, as Caroline called it; a delightful room on the other side of the hallway from the shop, where deep, button-back armchairs were grouped around an elegant, Georgian fireplace. Sleepy from the warmth of the fire, Holly sat back and listened while the others took it in turns to plan her future.

It would have been difficult to say which of them was the most enthusiastic. She was growing accustomed to John's quick, spontaneous suggestions, but Abigail could be relentless in the pursuit of an idea, and quiet Caroline, now sewing at a tapestry cushion-cover, was continually looking up from her work to make a point that the other two had overlooked. It was she who showed most concern for Holly's creature comforts.

"The roof may leak and the whole place need rethatching," she warned, after Abigail had completed a run-down — room by room — how she would decorate Rosemary Cottage.

"I know just the chap for that," John assured her.

"Mum and I could easily run-up

curtains — once we've measured for them," said Abigail. "And we often have furniture sales in Marlingham. If you let me know what you want I'll keep my eyes open."

"I've been wondering about advertising the bakery," said John. "We could have leaflets printed and distributed."

"A few posters around the town would help, too," said Abigail.

Holly felt a surge of panic. If I don't stop them now, she thought, the whole operation will actually start happening. And Brian doesn't even know about it, yet!

"I think," John Lorimer was saying thoughtfully, "it might be a good idea if I introduce you to a few people after church tomorrow. Have them in for a glass of sherry, perhaps."

"No!" said Holly decisively; and then, appalled at the effect that one small word had had upon them, stammered, "I'm sorry! I didn't mean to sound so rude. It's just that I'm not ready for all this, yet."

It was Caroline who saved her the effort of trying to explain further. "My dear, it's we who should apologise to you! Here we are — planning your whole life for you when all you want to do is to relax for a few hours. John, Abigail — not another word!"

"Only to say I'm sorry, too," said John, looking so contrite, Holly smiled at him forgivingly.

"And I'll put on some records," offered Abigail. "Something soothing!"

"That," said Holly gratefully, "would be wonderful."

And the next hour passed quietly enough; with the occasional collapse of a charred log into ashes and the rhythmic tick of the grandfather clock, behind John's chair, the only sounds to disturb the tranquillity of the music that Abigail had selected.

Next day, too, they kept their promise. Even to the extent of making a formal pact that none of them should be left alone with Holly for too long.

"That way," Abigail explained, "we'll make sure that we're all keeping to the agreement." Even when John suggested that he take Holly for a walk after they'd cleared away and washed up the lunch dishes, Abigail said she was coming too.

"Oh, I don't think *that's* necessary," her mother objected quickly.

"Yes, it is!" said Abbie firmly. "When he gets that dedicated look I don't trust my uncle an inch!"

In the event all four of them drove towards the wooded slopes of the Chilterns that Holly had first gazed at from the window of Rosemary Cottage.

"They're at their best in the autumn," said John.

They strode between the smooth, grey trunks of the beech trees, through drifts of dry, rustling leaves, and Holly felt the blood tingle in her cheeks.

"Now, you're really beginning to look like your name," said John Lorimer, as he helped her across the stepping-stones of a shallow brook, and they both balanced precariously in mid-stream.

"Prickly at the edges, d'you mean?" Holly laughed.

"No!" He shook her gently, and she felt the pressure of his arms through the cloth of her jacket. "Warm and glowing and alive!"

He, too, looked alive and surprisingly younger as he smiled down at her, his eyes brimming with merriment.

"Hurry up, you two!" called Abbie. "You're obstructing the highway!"

"Sorry!" And John led her carefully across the remaining stones.

There were buttered crumpets and fruit cake for tea, and Holly swore that her figure would be ruined. But at the same time she knew John Lorimer was right. She felt more alive than she had for weeks. Crazy to imagine she might be a country girl at heart! Feeling that now familiar sense of panic again, she declared that she must leave as soon as tea was over. Brian might have got back earlier than he'd expected.

This time John, Caroline and Abbie all

stood in the square to wave goodbye. And true to their promise no-one mentioned the bakery. It was Holly, leaning out of the window as she turned the ignition-key, who said "I'll be in touch — about you know what!"

As she let herself into the flat, the telephone was ringing.

"Holly, where have you been, for heaven's sake?" Clearly, Brian was in no mood for romantic small-talk.

"I thought you were away for the whole weekend," she countered.

"Obviously! And would you please answer my question."

"I've been to Marlingham."

"After all we'd decided? Holly, what on earth came over you?"

"Please let me explain, Brian. I really had no alternative."

"I'm afraid I find that rather difficult to believe."

"I'll tell you all about it tomorrow evening," she promised.

"Too late! I'm off to Manchester in

47

the morning. I'm only here now because I need clean shirts and socks."

Would marriage to Brian, she suddenly wondered, mean him always dashing from one end of Britain to the other, with herself handing out clean shirts and socks as he passed? To her horror she suddenly began to giggle — and couldn't stop.

"Holly, are you all right?"

"P-perfectly!"

"You don't sound it! Anyway, there are things we must clear up. I'm coming round."

"It's very late."

"Not as late as I've sometimes been," he reminded her. "And I can't stand this uncertainty. I must know what the situation is."

And he wasn't, Holly realised, the only one. What was the matter with her, that she was acting like a silly, vacillating schoolgirl, unable to make up her own mind?

"All right," she agreed. "But I have a busy day tomorrow, too, remember."

When, ten minutes later, she opened the door to him, she was surprised to see how tired he looked. Immediately she felt guilty and contrite.

"Come in and sit down. I'll get you a drink."

As she poured it she told him about John Lorimer's phone-call asking if she would see the bakery workforce. "It was the least I could do, Brian."

"Lorimer instigated the idea, I've no doubt. Anyway, I trust you've made the position crystal clear to them now."

"I've said I'll let them know definitely in a day or two."

"For heaven's sake, Holly, why prolong the agony? Why not tell them you're selling and that their future will depend upon the next owner?"

Her head came up. "But you haven't met them. They're such genuine, honest people."

"Implying what, exactly? That I'm not?"

"Don't be so ridiculous! Why are you so touchy tonight?"

They glared at each other, and then Brian put down his drink and crossed to her.

"Look!" He put his arm around her. "I've been trying to get you on the phone since midday. And I guessed you were at Marlingham. What's the situation down there, Holly? And I don't mean with your precious bakery staff. I mean with that fellow, Lorimer?"

"Don't be ridiculous!" she said again.

"I'm not being ridiculous! Some women find older men wildly attractive. Tell me just one thing, Holly. Do you or do you not want to marry me?"

"Of course, I do!" To her own ears, the words sounded over-emphatic. But they seemed to satisfy Brian.

"Well, that's something. I can see that you have a conscience about these people and their jobs, and the fact that I haven't is beside the point, I suppose. So why not put the bakery and the cottage on the market as we'd agreed, but stipulate that the purchaser must undertake to run the bakery and employ the old staff?"

50

There was only one thing that Holly was sure about just then; that she was far too tired to reach any new decisions. "I'll think about it," she promised. "But not now, Brian. We're both far too tired to talk sensibly."

"Who wants to be sensible?" he muttered. And his kiss, as he rose to go, made it clear that he was only leaving under protest. "You don't realise," he told her, "just how much I love you."

"I love you, too," she assured him, but still led him to the door.

4

IN spite of her exhaustion, Holly slept badly. When the telephone rang soon after seven, she was already making coffee.

"Sorry to be so early," said John Lorimer, "but I didn't know what time you left for your office. And it's important I speak to you as soon as possible."

Perhaps because she'd been afraid it would be Brian, urging her to consider his new plan, Holly felt a rush of relief. "Don't worry! I've been up for ages. What did you want to speak to me about?"

"Well, it's not that simple. I'd really much rather see you. I don't suppose there's the remotest chance of your getting the day off"

"Well," she hesitated, mentally assessing the work on hand. "I could manage the afternoon, I think. My editor has a meeting and won't need me."

"Lunch at one, then?" And he named a small, exclusive restaurant not far from her office.

She smiled to herself when she'd put down the phone, remembering Brian's words . . . 'These rustics are all the same. Get him away from his own environment and you'd soon be bored to tears!' Somehow, she doubted very much if that forecast would be proved correct. But it was difficult, even so, to imagine John in anything but his worn cords and baggy jacket!

Deciding upon the right clothes herself took longer than usual. Eventually, she chose a lightweight suit of pastel-shaded bouclé. Worn with a dark blouse it managed to look both smart and informal — just in case John did turn up in his country gear!

Arriving at the restaurant just after one, she felt a twinge of disappointment. He wasn't there! Then a tall figure unwound itself from a stool at the tiny bar in the foyer and came quickly towards her and she realised how completely mistaken Brian's assessment had been. John Lorimer, London style, was still quietly confident and at ease. With a cream-coloured, cashmere jersey he wore a finely checked, brown suit that showed the cut of an excellent tailor.

"Holly, how nice!" He shook her warmly by the hand, as if it was several weeks since they'd last met, instead of less than twenty-four hours.

When they were settled at a table and John had ordered their meal, showing a ready appreciation of both menu and wine list, Holly asked, "What did you want to talk to me about?"

"Let's enjoy our meal first, and then we'll talk." He studied her closely. "You look tired. As if you hadn't slept well."

"I didn't, actually." Although the urge to confide in him was strong, she said nothing about Brian's ultimatum.

"Life's rather difficult for you at the moment, isn't it?" he said sympathetically.

She nodded. "I feel as if I'm being torn in two. Up here there's Brian and our life together. I've a fascinating job with good prospects, and I love London. Theatres, concerts, exhibitions, all on my doorstep. Until a few days ago I thought that was all I wanted."

"And now there's Marlingham," he said, "offering a whole new set of values and a completely different way of life. I know just what you mean."

"You do?"

He crumbled a piece of bread while he gazed absentmindedly at the table-cloth. "I was a little like you, once. Fresh from university, a tiny flat not a stone's throw from here, a rewarding position in commerce with opportunities to travel, and friends galore."

"And a girl?" she asked. "Was there a special girl?"

He lifted his eyes and grinned at her. "Several!"

"Tell me about them!"

He shook his head. "Whose story *is* this? Anyway, the point of it is not to bore you with details of my youthful extravagances but to explain that I do understand just a little of what you're going through at the moment."

"You're not boring me," she insisted. "What happened?"

"Well, just when I was thoroughly enjoying life, my father died unexpectedly — at a very early age. He ran the bookshop I now have, as his father and grandfather had before him. Eventually, I knew I would take over from him — it was unthinkable that the business should go to anyone except a Lorimer — but I naturally hadn't expected it to be so soon. My mother was an invalid, and Caroline's husband, a wonderful man, only too willing to help out, caught some obscure tropical disease on a business trip to Africa and also died, leaving Caroline with a young, very demanding Abigail. Unlike you, I really had no choice."

"That was really tough," said Holly gently.

"Oh, don't be sorry for me! Things have worked out pretty well. I've just sent my second novel to my publisher — a dubious contribution to the field of whodunnits. I'm very happy in my shop and I'm accepted as a sober and sensible citizen of Marlingham. Almost a pillar, you might say, of the community."

There was a barely perceptible note of self-mockery in his voice as he made the last remark, and Holly asked, "So, no regrets?"

He gave her a smile of rare sweetness. "Now and then, perhaps. When someone like you comes along, blowing away the cobwebs, shaking me out of my routine. Then I may think of what might have been and of those special girls you mentioned. Not that I can remember any one of them better than the others — so it was probably as well I wasn't tempted into matrimony!"

Holly laughed. "You're talking as if you were Marlingham's oldest resident!"

"Well, I must say I was beginning to feel like him! Until the other week, in fact, when Fate offered me a whole new project to grapple with."

"The bakery?"

"Exactly! Last night, after you'd gone

and the embargo had been lifted, the three of us sat round the fire and really got down to working out what could be done. And I haven't enjoyed anything so much for a long time."

"Bread would certainly be a change from books," Holly said thoughtfully.

"It's not the product so much — though a loaf of freshly baked bread is certainly a thing of beauty, just as much as a book. It's the challenge of setting up a new business. And Abbie, as you must have noticed, has a very active and original mind. Caroline was her usual, sensible self, never hesitating to point out the impracticality of some of our ideas. We talked about it until well after midnight, and then we reached a unanimous decision." He paused to draw breath.

"Which was?" asked Holly impatiently.

"Why don't we run the bakery for you? It's asking a lot to suggest you give up your job, especially as you enjoy it so much, to tackle something that you might not like and might be a disaster, anyway, leaving you high and dry in a small market town. We'd make the whole thing strictly legal, of course, and I'm pretty sure, as I told you previously, that we could raise sufficient local support to provide the financial backing." He paused and looked at her expectantly. "What do you say?"

It was a question that he needn't have asked. Holly's eyes were sparkling with excitement. "I think it's a splendid idea! And so will Brian, when I tell him about it."

John's expression became guarded. "Yes, I suppose his approval would be necessary."

"We do plan to marry," she pointed out. "Actually, his idea was for me to sell the bakery and Rosemary Cottage to someone who would guarantee to run it, *and* employ the old staff."

"Did he now?" said John thoughtfully. "And you think he won't mind you not selling after all?"

"I don't see why he should. It would simply mean we'd have to have a mortgage when we married, instead of buying a house outright."

John Lorimer put back his head and roared with laughter. "There speaks the carefree, single girl! Few responsibilities and little need for domestic economy. Being able to start married life without a mortgage must be like winning the pools these days! It could mean a great deal to you and Brian, you know."

"I suppose so," said Holly slowly. She was remembering that Brian, in fact, had never positively suggested marriage until after they'd known about Great-aunt Gertrude's bequest.

"To get back to the bakery," said John, "we would like you to be able to use a veto, if you wanted to stop us doing something you didn't approve of. But Abbie, Caroline and I would be responsible for the day-to-day running."

"And what about the cottage?" Holly asked. "Would someone be living in that?"

He hesitated. "Actually, we saw you popping down at weekends, just to keep

60

in touch with developments."

"Oh!"

"You don't think Brian would approve?"

"He doesn't rule my entire life," Holly protested, an indignant flush creeping into her cheeks.

"Of course not," he said comfortably. "But there does happen to be an extremely fine golf-course only a few miles away if he felt like coming too."

Holly glanced at him suspiciously. How had he guessed that Brian was a keen golfer? But his face was devoid of expression.

"As a matter of fact," he said blandly, "I enjoy a game there myself, on occasion."

"You wouldn't," Holly pointed out, "have much time for leisure activities if you were running a bakery as well as a bookshop."

"The time to worry," he told her gravely, "would be when customers began to complain of crumbs in the books!"

Holly laughed. "And when do you aim to start this dramatic double life?"

"As soon as possible. As a matter of fact

there are one or two possible investors coming in to play bridge with Caroline this evening. If you're agreeable I'll tell them about the bakery and sound out their reactions."

"Good idea!" she said, stifling her immediate reaction of disappointment that he wouldn't, apparently, be spending the evening with her.

Perhaps her face had given her away because he suddenly put out his hand to cover hers. "Now, let's forget about mundane matters like bakeries and pretend that you're my beautiful princess, and I'm just a simple, country bumpkin up in London for the day."

"Simple is hardly the word I'd use!"

He grinned. "I said we were pretending! Anyway, what does my princess suggest we do this afternoon?"

"My bumpkin has nothing in mind?"

He thought for a moment. "Well, being a bookish sort of bumpkin, he'd rather like to visit the Charing Cross Road where he's heard the shops are full of books. Or would that bore her royal highness to distraction?"

"The princess can read, believe it or not!"

"Good! And *she* can decide what to do after that."

Holly wrinkled her forehead. "St. James's Park, to feed the ducks?"

His face lit up. "Would you really like to do that? Or are you just indulging me?"

"Honestly, I'd love it. My grandfather used to take me there on Sunday afternoons when I was a little girl, and I haven't been for ages."

He considered her with a quizzical eye. "I'm quite sure you were a dreadful tomboy when you were small."

"With two older brothers I didn't have much option."

"And where's your family now?"

"My parents emigrated to New Zealand with my eldest brother. I'm going out to see them next summer. But my grandfather's still going strong and living with my brother, down in Hereford. We've always been a very close family."

"I wish I'd known you when you were small. I see you as a little girl with a gamin hair-cut and very expressive eyes. And rather shy. Am I right?"

"Painfully shy, but otherwise — wrong. I had pigtails and a brace on my teeth!"

"So had I! The brace, if not the pigtails!"

The rest of the afternoon was as carefree as Holly could wish. Hand-in-hand — 'bumpkin's a little scared of all these people!' — they wandered from shop to shop down the Charing Cross Road. In several, Holly was interested to observe, John was known and obviously liked and respected.

By the time they reached the park the shadows were lengthening. Somewhere a bonfire was smouldering, and the scent of chrysanthemums spiced the air. The ducks were already settling for the night.

"Past their bedtime," said Holly. "Maybe they won't be hungry, now."

"Ducks," John Lorimer assured her, "are always hungry. Watch this!"

He opened the bag of buns they had brought, and immediately convoys of birds materialised out of the rushes and converged upon them. Soon the bag was empty.

"Look at that old boy! He was probably here when you and your grandfather came!" John aimed a last strategic morsel at a bedraggled-looking mallard on the edge of the throng. "There! That's your lot! And I hope you don't all have indigestion tonight." He turned to Holly. "I can't tell you how much I've enjoyed myself today. Thank you, princess!"

"I'm no princess. Any more than you're a country bumpkin!"

"But we've had a wonderful day pretending."

"I've loved every second."

He bent his head and, instinctively, she tilted back her own; but he paused, gave her a brief smile and said, "Come along, I'll put you in a taxi."

As if they'd been queuing at the gates, the park was suddenly crowded with home-going office-workers. "The

65

"nearest tube will do," she assured him. "I shall have plenty of company."

But he insisted upon calling a taxi and paying the driver. "I'll telephone soon," he promised.

In the taxi she found herself wondering if John Lorimer had intended to kiss her in the park and, if so, what had made him change his mind. Pleasurably, she imagined the feel of his lips upon her own and then scolded herself for her undisciplined feelings. She was, after all, engaged to Brian.

5

TELLING Brian about the proposed new plans for the bakery wasn't too difficult. That evening, as he often did, he called in at her flat.

"I saw John Lorimer, today," she told him as a preliminary, pouring him a generous drink.

"Again?"

"He — had to come up to town on business and afterwards, we had lunch together." She avoided mentioning their visit to the bookshops and to the park.

"So you told him that we'd decided to sell the cottage and the bakery to someone who was willing to operate the business and employ the old staff?"

"Yes — he thought it was a most commendable idea on your part."

"I'm flattered. Did he suggest buying it himself?"

She was astonished how near to the

truth he was. "Not to buy it, but to run it for me."

"*Us,*" he corrected.

"Us," she agreed dutifully.

"And what would we get out of an arrangement like that? What proportion of the takings?"

She stared at him in open-mouthed astonishment. He was right, of course, to be so down-to-earth and business-like. She should have found out, herself, exactly what the financial arrangements were to be. But it had simply never occurred to her to raise the question with John Lorimer. And there had been so many other things to talk about.

Brian suddenly left the chair in which he'd been lounging and came to sit beside her on the settee. "You see, kitten, you do need me! Admit it now, you haven't a clue about the financial side of the deal."

She didn't think she was *that* hopeless, but she was grateful that his demand for detail seemed to have been deflected by the enormity of her ignorance. She said nothing.

He smiled at her fondly. "Once we're married, my sweet, you can leave all mundane matters like that to me."

His arm had been lying along the back of the settee, behind her head, his fingers idly caressing her hair, and now they began to pull out the pins which held it in the smooth, elegant pleat she wore during the day.

"Brian!" she protested feebly, for she knew that this was the preliminary to the love-making that, so far, she had managed to control.

But his hand was already entwined in the thick strands of her hair, pulling back her head to expose the slender column of her throat. His lips pressed lingeringly into the hollow at the base of her neck while, with his other hand, he began to undo the collar of her blouse.

"Brian!" Admittedly, he took his hand away, but only to force her body upright so that he could more easily press his lips upon hers. Very gently his fingers began to glide up and down her spine and, in spite of her determination, she felt her resistance begin to weaken. Not for the first time, she thought that he understood the demands of her body far better than she did herself. Resolutely, she pulled her mouth away.

"Brian, we'll soon be married. Let's wait until then."

Abruptly his fingers stilled and he lifted his head to look down at her. She felt desire drain away from her own body, leaving her limp and exhausted, and guessed that it must be the same for him.

"It's not as simple as that," he told her. "Although it *could be.* It's just a matter of choice. Give up this ridiculous notion of hanging on to the bakery. Or marry me!"

She wondered if he had deliberately roused her senses so that he could deliver this ultimatum with greater force.

"But Brian, why must I choose?" she protested. "We love each other. That's all that matters."

He moved to the other end of the scttcc. "There speaks my naïve little girl! Haven't you thought about the rising price of property?"

Not until this afternoon! she thought.

"I won't bother you with the sordid details," he continued, "but to live in the life-style to which we're both accustomed, and in an area we like, would cost a great deal of money."

"Why can't I just move in with you? Or you with me?"

"Because, my sweet, they're both one-person flats, and we'd be hideously cramped."

"It could be fun!"

"For the first week or two, perhaps. No, Holly, that's one thing I'm determined about — that we should begin our married life with everything we need."

"But, Brian, I wouldn't need much," she coaxed. "Why couldn't we be married at Christmas?"

"You know that Colin and Tessa want us to spend it with them in Switzerland."

"It could be the perfect honeymoon!"

"A honeymoon with two other people?

What's happened to your romantic spirit?
But we could certainly have a super
holiday."

"And meantime I let John Lorimer
handle the bakery?" she countered swiftly.

He frowned. "Are you blackmailing
me?"

"No more than you were blackmailing
me!"

"My little girl isn't so naïve after all!"
He got to his feet and began to pace about
the room. "Certainly the property would
fetch a better price if it were to be sold as
a going concern. Provided you get a good
lawyer to handle things our way, it might
not be such a bad idea after all."

"There's Mr. Boucher," she said swiftly,
delighted that he seemed to have given
in with such good grace. "Great-aunt
Gertrude's lawyer. I'm sure he would
represent me."

"Perhaps I'd better have a word with
him first."

"By all means, if you want to." She
was determined not to damage this new,
almost cooperative attitude of his. "We'll

see him together."

"And Switzerland?" he asked.

"Will be lovely for Christmas," she agreed gaily, subduing the presentiment that Brian's idea of a perfect holiday foursome was unlikely to be hers. She'd face that problem when the time came.

John Lorimer rang her that evening soon after Brian had left.

"Just to let you know that things look very hopeful. Of the half dozen people I've approached, suggesting they might like to invest in the bakery, five have shown interest. So has the sixth, but he's just put his spare capital into a chicken-farm for his son. I've made appointments to see the five hopefuls during the next couple of days."

"Great!" said Holly. "And Brian has given his approval, too."

There was a barely perceptible pause. "And your plans for marrying? You're still going ahead with those?"

"Postponed for the moment," said Holly lightly. "You were quite right about the mortgage!"

"Well, at least you'll have more time to come and see us," said John. "And will you let me have the name of your lawyer? He must get together with mine and make sure that your interests are protected — just in case the whole project's a ghastly flop. Not that it will be!"

Holly felt a profound sense of relief that Brian's attitude had been so completely unjustified.

"Sleep well!" said John. "And try and get down for the weekend for a progress report."

6

ONCE more Brian was away on business, so that Holly, with a clear conscience, could go down to Marlingham for the weekend. She stayed with the Lorimers again, but made the point that she intended to make Rosemary Cottage habitable as soon as possible.

"I can't keep on accepting your hospitality like this," she told John soon after she'd arrived on Friday evening.

"No earthly reason why not. We all love having you. But it would be better for the cottage to be lived in than to stay empty. By the way, we've called an investors' meeting, if that's not too grand a title, for tomorrow morning to find out what has to be done to the bakery in the way of repairs."

"When do you aim to start?" asked Holly.

"Just as soon as we can get the business side sorted out and the oven working. And we shall expect you to come down for the official opening, of course."

"Are we to have a ceremony?"

"Naturally! Abbie loves any excuse for a party, and this one could be good for trade. A cold buffet, with everything made in the bakery and guests able to place an order on the spot."

"And what," asked Holly, "is this magnificent new company to be called?"

"What do you suggest?"

"Why not 'Baxters'? That's what everyone will call it whatever name *we* give it! 'Baxters for your Home-Baked Bread'. I can just see it on the side of the van."

She looked at him questioningly. "We do have a van, I suppose?"

"Of course we have. Two, to be precise. One, horse-drawn, for the local deliveries. And a motorised effort, that Buckie's found in Aylesbury, for anything over a couple of miles. Both need painting up."

"Whose going to drive the horse?"

"Abbie, would you believe! She rather fancies herself clopping down the country lanes, stopping for sandwiches and nosebags under the trees! Having ridden all her life she reckons it should be easy enough. Mike Hawkins, our vet., is letting us have the horse a rather elderly mare called Daisy Belle, but still capable of light duties. She's pulled a brewer's dray all her working life so she should know all the wrinkles."

"Let's hope Abbie does! Tell me more about this investors' meeting. It sounds slightly formidable."

"That's the last thing it will be. The company, in its official capacity, doesn't exist yet. It's more of a little social gathering because we thought you might like to meet everybody."

"Didn't anyone think we might be biting off more than we could chew?"

"Well, no, because most of them remember the bakery as having been a very flourishing concern."

"They really feel we can't lose," said

Abbie, coming into the room at that moment.

Her uncle looked at her with mock severity. "Would you mind touching wood, crossing your fingers and generally not tempting Providence when you make a remark like that, Abbie? The *Titanic* was considered unsinkable, you know."

"Stop trying to sound like an ancient uncle! You know perfectly well you're as confident as I am."

"Well, deep down in my bones I am, but it's part of my carefully preserved image to try and seem like a restraining influence upon you!"

"Well, all I can say is that your image has been slipping a bit lately — you're looking younger every day, and Mum's noticed it, too. She thinks it's all due to Holly and the bakery."

"Abbie!" said her uncle sharply. "That's enough!" And this time, thought Holly, he means it. "Tell Holly about our benefactors," he added in a milder tone.

"Right!" said Abbie unabashed, and perching herself upon the arm of her uncle's chair held up one finger. "First of all, there's Mike Hawthorne, the vet. — he's the one that's giving us Daisy Belle. He's tall, dark and ugly, and all animals love him on sight!"

"Quite a few humans, too," said John slyly.

"Come to think of it," said Abbie, rather too casually, "he usually does have a clutch of gawping females hanging around him."

Holly caught John's eye, and he gave a barely perceptible flicker of one eyelid. "Not Abbie, of course!" he said.

Abbie tossed her head. "I don't hang around any man!" She held up another finger. "Then there's Dr. Bellamy — he's coming in because of the health of the community. Or so he says! Personally, I think it's because he adores good food! That leaves Mr. Bartlett, a farmer, Mr. George Smith, the owner of the Royal Oak, and Mr. Johnson, the agent for the Jarvis estates."

"But not Sir Henry Jarvis himself unfortunately," said John.

"Sir Henry Jarvis? Haven't I heard that name before somewhere?" Holly asked.

"The odds are about a hundred to one in his favour," said John, "that every time you clean your teeth or wash your face you're using one of his products. He has his country seat about a mile outside Marlingham. But seldom visits the town because it doesn't happen to lie between here and London."

"Have you ever met him?" Holly asked.

"Once, when he turned up in my shop because he'd heard I'd got a first edition he wanted. He's not married, and apparently collects books and objets d'art like most people in his position collect steam-yachts and fast cars. He invited me to go and see his library at the manor sometime, but I've never done anything about it. It's not the sort of place you drop in to, on the off-chance of him being at home. Horses are his other preoccupation, I understand."

"However wealthy he is, he'll still have

to eat bread," said Abbie. "So, why not ours? I think I'll call on him, if you won't. On a strictly business footing, of course," she added virtuously, "not to entice him with my feminine charms! Anyway, I've just remembered Mum sent me in to tell you supper's ready!"

"Now, she tells us!" said her uncle.

The meal was as delicious, the company as friendly, as Holly had remembered. But this time the taboo had been lifted — talk about the bakery was not only permitted, it was encouraged. When, eventually, they all made their way to bed she was as excited about the project as the Lorimers. And tomorrow, she reminded herself she must buy a few essentials for Rosemary Cottage. Nothing too expensive, just some basic pieces of furniture.

Holly was used to meetings; from formal, round-the-table conferences to informal discussions that could still decide important policy, but the gathering in John Lorimer's study next morning was something quite new to her.

"When do we start?" she asked John, when she'd been introduced to half a dozen or so men, including Mr. Peechey, John's lawyer.

"Start what?"

"The meeting, of course!"

"Bless the girl! Were you expecting to take the minutes? I'm afraid it isn't that sort of a meeting."

"But shouldn't we ask if they have any questions?"

"Look around you! Mr. Peechey, as you can see, is deep in conversation with Ralph Bartlett and Dr. Bellamy. You may be quite sure that they are having the whole arrangement explained to them in detail. As soon as they move away someone else will take their place. None of these people are given to public discussion and argument but, believe me, they're as shrewd as they come. There's the other point, too, that they won't want to hurt our feelings — particularly yours — by asking awkward questions about interest rates and payment dates, but they won't mind asking Mr. Peechey."

"John, what *about* interest rates and repayment dates," asked Holly in some alarm. "What if we can't meet them?"

"Now, don't worry! The whole object of this arrangement is to take the responsibility off your shoulders. All you have to be is a charming figurehead!"

"I'm not sure that I like that much. There's such a sense of purpose about you all, I feel I want to be part of it."

"Well, of course you are. If it wasn't for you, remember, none of this would be happening. You're supposed to feel privileged — not deprived!"

"All right. I'll do my best to be nothing but a figurehead."

"Charming figurehead, I said!" When he spoke to her in that warm, intimate fashion it was as if she were the only person in the room who mattered. Where Brian, she thought, used the sheer, physical magnetism of his body to attract a woman, this man's appeal lay in the quiet strength of his personality. A girl could easily find herself in love with him before she knew it, Holly thought, and then told herself not to be so fanciful.

"And what is my charming figurehead worrying about now?" he enquired.

For a moment she was tempted to take advantage of the question to say — 'she was just thinking that you should marry some beautiful, intelligent woman and have lots of lovely children with dark eyes and black curls,' — but she knew instinctively that the remark would bring their easy relationship to an abrupt end. More than most men, he would hate to be told what he should do. So instead she said, "As I'm going to be living in Rosemary Cottage at the weekends I must furnish it with a few basic necessities. Have you any idea where I might find some oldish furniture that wouldn't cost the earth?"

"The Glory Hole in the High Street," he said promptly. "A treasure trove of castes that turn out to be exactly what other people are looking for. Sometimes quite valuable pieces."

"I don't want to spend too much time or money," she explained, "because I shan't be staying there indefinitely. I think I can safely say it will never be Brian's choice of somewhere to live."

"No, I can see that. Well," he gave her one of his quizzical smiles, "we must enjoy you while we have the opportunity. And, talking of enjoyment, here comes Mike Hawkins. Have you ever seen a more expressive face?"

A giant of a man with a crop of thick, black hair, grey eyes and the tanned skin of someone perpetually exposed to all weathers was making his way towards them. As he came he called out greetings to some, clapped others on their shoulders and generally exuded a spirit of jovial friendliness. 'Tall, dark and ugly' had been an apt description of Abbie's, thought Holly. In repose, this man's features would be like granite — the nose a craggy beak, the chin jutting strongly under the firm mouth, the high cheek-bones lending a faintly puckish quality to the deep-set eyes. But when he smiled or spoke — which was for most of the time — he showed a set of white, even teeth in a lop-sided grin, and his eyes sparkled with humour.

"Delighted to meet you, m'dear," he told Holly, pumping her hand vigorously. "Now I understand why this bookworm of ours has at last turned into a normal, human being!"

"The important thing to realise about Mike, right from the start," said John blandly, "is that he can be guaranteed to embarrass you wherever you may be and with whomever you may be! In a moment, he'll probably point out that I'm wearing odd socks!"

"Now, who would be wanting to cast down their eyes at your great feet while there's someone as charming as Miss Sandford to look at, up here? And talking of charm, where has young Abigail hidden herself?"

"In the kitchen, dispensing beer or sherry. And not in the least hidden."

"What more can a man ask? Abbie and a foaming tankard! But a pleasure I must postpone for the moment I'm afraid. A cow at Hilltops Farm requires my assistance with a calf she's bearing. I'll just pay my respects and be on my way. Look forward to seeing you again soon, Miss Sandford. Or may I, like everyone else around here, call you Holly? Cheerio, John, don't forget I'm promised the first bun off the conveyor belt, or whatever!"

"Just the person for Abbie, I would think," said Holly, as she watched Mike shoulder his way easily through the crowded room.

"I think so. Caroline thinks so. I'm sure Mike, himself thinks so. But try telling Abbie! She has a will of her own, my niece."

"Give her time," Holly advised. "She'll realise what's good for her in the end."

"I hope you're right. Now, come and mingle a little more, and then we'll call the meeting to order and tell it to go home! Then we can go and peer into the Glory Hole to our hearts' content."

The afternoon meeting was, if that were possible, even more informal. It took place in the front room of Rosemary Cottage with the participants seated upon the various pieces of furniture Holly had just acquired.

There was a small fireside chair that she had firmly declared would 'do for now!' even when John had drawn her attention to a pair of reasonably priced, winged armchairs covered in faded, but clean, chintz.

"But surely you agree that they would look perfect either side of your inglenook?"

"Far too perfect! If I'm not careful, Rosemary Cottage will take possession of me."

"Explain yourself!" And he'd sat down in one of the chairs under discussion, so that she could do nothing else but occupy the other.

"Well, it's obviously the sort of cottage that would be fascinating to decorate and furnish. And heaven to live in, when it was. But places like that can take a hold on you — and, when you consider that I'm going to marry Brian, that would be a fatal thing to happen."

"Ah yes, Brian! For the moment I'd forgotten him. All right, no nice chairs! But what about a table? You're not going to eat off the floor, I take it?"

"A card-table, possibly two," she'd conceded. "One in the living-room and another in the kitchen. There's a water-heater and an old cooker there, already, I noticed."

"Don't forget you can always pop things into the bakery oven, once it's going," he'd reminded her. "And before you buy yourself that hideously uncomfortable looking camp-bed over there, Caroline has a divan she's trying to find a home for."

"Honestly? I must say, I do like to sleep comfortably."

The total result of her purchases had been the fireside chair, an upright kitchen chair, two card-tables, a roll of coconut-matting, an electric kettle, some odd but unchipped cups and saucers, a sweeping brush and a cheap lamp. The last, in spite of a Victorian oil-lamp they'd discovered just before leaving and which had sorely tempted her.

"But it would look quite out of place in a modern flat," she'd said firmly, "and I know I wouldn't want to part with it, once it was mine."

"Curtains?" John had suggested, hovering outside the door of a draper's, next door to the Glory Hole. "It wouldn't take Caroline a minute to run them up on her machine."

"No, thank you. The ones left by the previous owner will do quite well. I'll rinse them through this evening."

And now, after a quick sandwich, they were deep into plans for the bakery.

"There's more to be done than I'd expected," Mr. Baxter admitted. "Quite a few tiles off the roof and the back wall needs replastering. The oven itself isn't too bad, but some of the tiles and bricks will need replacing. Once that's all taken care of we can give it a coat of paint ourselves. Save a bit of money that way."

"Talking of money" said Mrs. Baxter,

"if we're going to make pies, as you suggest, Mrs. Forbes, we should have some equipment for cutting the pastry, as soon as we can afford it. By hand it will take a long time. Not," she added hastily, "that I don't think it's a splendid thing to make pies. They'll go down well. We shall need some sacks of special flour, of course."

"Right!" John made a note on his pad — 'special flour and pastry-cutting equipment'. "We'll make that a number one priority, Mrs. Baxter. Any other points?"

"As I understand it," said Mr. Baxter, "you want to take orders from the village shops around, as well as the townsfolk?"

John nodded. "Yes, I've already written to the stores concerned, explaining what we're doing and asking them if they'd like to place their orders."

"You don't think," said Mr. Baxter cautiously, "that it might be better to get established in the town first, and then go out to the villages?"

"I take your point, Mr. Baxter," said John, "but I think from what you've told me about our capacity that we should be able to manage both. As you know, we've borrowed money from some of the local people, but on the understanding that we start to repay it by a certain date. We shall only be able to do this if we spread our net as widely as possible. Eventually, when we've established ourselves, we may even be able to build a second oven."

Mr. Baxter brightened visibly. "That's very good news!"

Albert raised his hand to catch John's attention. "I suppose we'll be keeping some pigs, Mr. Lorimer? To eat up any stale bread we may have left. There's a sty round the back," he added. "A coat of whitewash is all it would need."

John looked dubious. "I wonder if we shouldn't wait a while before adding to our responsibilities? After all, with careful planning we shouldn't have too much stale bread. What do you think, Mr. Baxter?"

"Well, we always did have pigs in the old days, Mr. Lorimer, and very profitable they were, too. But perhaps we should wait a while, as you suggest. We can always sell any stale loaves to the butcher," he pointed out to Albert, "for his sausages."

"Well, I'll get the sty ready, just in case," said Albert philosophically.

And Holly had the distinct impression that, left to him, it would soon have an occupant.

"When d'you think the bakery should be ready?" John asked Mr. Baxter.

"As long as we can get the repairs done quickly, two or three weeks I should say. We shall have to get a specialist in to repair the oven. By that time Buckie should have got the van roadworthy, and the horse will be used to the cart. Still going to drive her, are you, Miss Abbie?"

"Rather!" said Abbie, from where she sat in the window-seat, knees up to chin. "Actually, I thought I'd take her for a little ride tomorrow morning. Mike says she's broken to the saddle. I won't actually put her between the shafts, but if I work her for a few hours every day we'll soon get to know each other. What do you think?"

"A very good idea, miss. You'll find her in that big field where the allotments used to be during the war."

"Miss Abbie won't remember the war, Bill," his wife chided.

"But I know the field he means, Mrs. Baxter," Abbie assured her. "There's a clump of willows in the middle of it."

"That's the one! Take an apple and she'll come easy enough."

The conversation moved on then to discussion about the opening ceremony. With only half of her attention, Holly listened to Mrs. Baxter agreeing that it would be best if Caroline made the pie fillings at home and had them brought down to the bakery for Mrs. Baxter to put into the pastry cases. The other half was registering the fact that the living-room curtains were far shabbier than she'd remembered. Perhaps she'd been foolish to reject John's suggestion that Caroline should run up some more. Once the naked light-bulbs were lit, the present ones would give scant protection from the gaze of anyone coming down Bun Lane after dark. Remembering the lovely, Victorian lamp, she wished, after all, that she'd bought it. Placed in the window of the living-room, its soft glow would have shone out across the garden to light her way up the path.

She suddenly became aware that silence had fallen and that everyone was gazing at her expectantly. "How about trying out that new electric kettle and making some tea?" John suggested, and not, she had the impression, for the first time.

"I'll help!" Abbie uncurled herself from the window-seat.

Soon afterwards the little meeting broke up, and Holly accompanied the Baxters and Albert into the yard where Buckie was already back underneath his van, crooning contentedly to himself.

"I was wondering," Mrs. Baxter paused by the bakery door, which Holly now knew was called a 'gossip' door, "if it wouldn't be nice to have a tub of plants outside in the summer? There's that old millstone that's been there longer than I can remember crying out to have something on top of it."

"Splendid idea!" said Holly, and quickly averted her gaze from the decaying vegetation choking the garden of the cottage. She must try and do something about it before long.

When she went back indoors she found that the others had already swept out the living-room and were attempting to arrange her bits and pieces to the best possible advantage. But with little success.

"Holly, they look terrible!" said Abigail frankly. "Not a bit in keeping with the cottage. Why don't you . . .

"Abbie!" Her uncle raised his hand. "Holly knows it looks terrible but she has very good reasons for wanting it that way."

"She *has*, has she?" Abbie was frankly disbelieving.

"At least your bed should be comfortable," said Caroline with her usual tact. "I've made it up for you in the front bedroom. The sheets and blankets were part of the deal."

Holly thanked her warmly and then allowed her eye to wander around the room. She knew what they must all be thinking, and seeing perhaps, in their minds' eye, the glint of firelight on brass and copper, fresh curtains at the window, pewter plates on an old oak dresser; everything, in fact, as a room in an old cottage should look.

"Right!" said John, breaking the silence. "If we're all finished, we might as well go. The kind people minding the shop will need a break. You're coming with us, aren't you, Holly? There's plenty for you to do."

It was more a statement of fact than a question, and Holly looked at him gratefully. The spartan state of affairs at Rosemary Cottage might be of her own choosing, but to be left with them just now was the last thing she wanted!

And, as John had said, there was plenty to do. Suppliers of flour and yeast and other ingredients had to be contacted, and estimates made of their requirements from the old order books that Bill Baxter had produced, carefully wrapped in a piece of oilskin cloth.

"You're the secretary bird," John told her. "We'll isolate you in my study so you won't have any distractions."

And there she stayed with an ancient typewriter and a supply of paper and envelopes until she was called for a glass of sherry just before supper.

"And what have the rest of you been doing?" she demanded, faintly surprised that she hadn't even been brought a cup of tea.

"Oh, this and that!" said Caroline vaguely. "Abbie's been helping me in the kitchen. John had to go out."

By the time they had cleared away the meal it was late, and Holly didn't object when John offered to see her home. She wasn't at all sure that she fancied Bun Lane in total darkness.

But, surprisingly, it wasn't. As they turned into it, John's hand guiding her over the ruts, she saw a glimmer of light at the far end, where Rosemary Cottage was a dark hump against the starry sky.

"I must have left a light on," she said. "Careless of me!" But the light was coming, she soon realised, not from one of the naked bulbs in any of the rooms, but from a lamp set in the sitting-room window and sending a shaft of light down the path. She stopped and looked up at John.

"It's that Victorian lamp from the Glory Hole, isn't it?"

"I went back for it," he admitted. "But we'll return it on Monday, if you really insist. Tonight I thought you might like to see how useful it is in the cottage."

"Useful! It's miraculous!"

She fitted her key into the lock, and they went into the tiny hall. John pushed open the door of the sitting-room, and she stood, speechless, on the threshold, her eyes widening at the transformation. It wasn't only the soft, luminous glow of the lamp — it was the crisp, chintz curtains drawn back on either side of it, the winged armchairs beside the inglenook where the fire still smouldered, the colourful rug on the tiled floor, the gate-legged table folded back against the wall and the deep, vibrant pink of the cyclamen in the copper bowl that she had last seen in Caroline's parlour.

"We didn't want to interfere," said John at her elbow, "but when we saw your face after the meeting we knew we couldn't leave you here as it was. You looked like a small child whose mother has said, 'no jam for tea for the next six weeks!' It only took Caroline and Abbie half an hour to run up the curtains, and all the furniture can go back to the Glory Hole when you leave. Just look upon it as a stage set for a theatrical production. When the play is over you can simply leave it all behind you and go on to your next part."

Suddenly, the room with all its warm,

golden beauty was nothing but a blur. The tears were pouring down Holly's cheeks.

"Here, have this!" A large handkerchief was thrust into her hand and she was held firmly against the friendly warmth of John's tweed jacket. "I'm sorry, Holly! Obviously it was a mistake. We shouldn't have interfered."

At that, she pushed herself away from him by the simple expedient of pressing her hands hard against his chest, although his arms still held her lightly. Vigorously, she shook her head. "That's not why I'm crying! I'm just so t-t-touched and . . . g-grateful!"

"That's all right then," he said in a matter of fact voice, as if that was the end of the matter. "For a moment I thought I'd have to take the lot back to the Glory Hole tonight!"

Holly mopped her eyes, blew her nose and smiled a watery but happy smile. "You're so sweet to me!"

A lock of hair had fallen into his eyes, and with his arms around her there was nothing he could do about it. Impulsively, she reached up and smoothed it back, and then gently ran her finger down the side of his cheek to the edge of his mouth. Perhaps because words were quite inadequate to express her appreciation of his kindness and perception, she found she was suddenly on tiptoe, her mouth reaching for his.

"Holly, my dear!" His arms tightened, and then his lips, warm and demanding, were upon hers, and they stood, folded closely in each other's arms. Instinctively feeling her whole being respond to a tumultuous tide of happiness, Holly brought her hand up behind his head, the easier to keep his mouth where it was.

Perhaps it was the movement that broke the spell. Perhaps, she thought later, there had been no spell as far as he was concerned. His hands dropped to his side and he moved away from her. There was a tiny silence, broken only by the hiss of the logs in the hearth, and then he said, "Well, goodnight, Holly! Sleep well!" And was gone, the front door shutting firmly behind him.

Holly was left, near to tears, with the sobering realisation that it was she who had initiated the embrace. She, who had reached up to him in what must have seemed an obvious invitation. And clearly it had meant nothing to him. Just part of the service, in fact, along with furnishing her sitting-room and taking care of her creature comforts. What must he think of her? Gone, now, was that feeling of intense happiness; that joyful elation such as she'd never experienced before, even when Brian had been at his most passionate.

Brian! She'd completely forgotten about him. In spirit, if not in fact, she'd certainly been unfaithful to him tonight. How would she feel when she saw him again? And, even more to the point, how would she feel when she met John, face to face, next morning?

7

"I'M just off to ride Daisy Belle round her field," announced Abbie next morning when Holly arrived at the Book Shop.

"Need any help?" Holly asked.

"No, thanks. I'm just telling you, like people should when they go climbing in the mountains!"

"Abbie! If you feel like that then I really ought to come."

"No, I'm only joking. Mike says she's safe as houses. He wouldn't let me ride her if she wasn't."

"A very nice man is Mike," said Holly staunchly.

"So everyone keeps telling me!"

"In that case," said Holly, "I'll save my breath." Nor was she particularly well-equipped to offer advice, anyway. Since last night and the startling effect of John's kiss, her mind had been in a turmoil. Was she falling in love with him? An older, but undeniably attractive man? Or was her reaction born of the gratitude she'd felt for his understanding of her needs?

I shall have to take my cue from him, she'd decided, before falling into a fitful sleep. If his attitude towards her was as it had always been — cheerful, almost avuncularly affectionate as he was to Abbie — then she would put the whole occurrence out of her mind. Or try to. Certainly, she would make sure that it never happened again.

She had slept late, hurriedly made coffee and toast on the old cooker in the kitchen, finding it surprisingly efficient, and then walked quickly up to the market square. But neither John nor Caroline were there.

"Gone to church," Abbie had explained before telling Holly of her own plans. So, after she'd watched Abbie drive away in her old two-seater, a bag of apples and a saddle and bridle on the seat beside her, Holly settled down to complete the clerical work she'd begun on the previous night.

About half an hour later, the telephone rang.

"Is that you, Lorimer?" a brisk male voice enquired as soon as she'd lifted the receiver.

"He's not here, I'm afraid. Can I take a message? I'm Holly Sandford, and I shall be here for the rest of the day."

"Message wouldn't do much good under the circumstances. May be too late. M'name's Jarvis and I have a horse called Grey Dawn. Thoroughbred. Mr. Lorimer, so my agent tells me, has a niece called Abigail. Correct?"

"Correct!"

"Well, I've just seen both of them heading due north across my paddock — and going at a devil of lick! Foolhardy speed, I would have thought, although Miss Abigail did seem to be handling her remarkably well. Even if she hadn't bothered to put on a saddle!"

Holly sat down abruptly.

"Still there?" enquired the voice. And,

when Holly gave a feeble affirmative, added, "Wondered if Lorimer could throw any light on the matter. Not accustomed to people borrowing my horses without so much as a by-your-leave."

"Does there happen to be a clump of willows in the field where your horse was grazing?" Holly asked.

"There is, indeed."

"Then I'm afraid Abigail must have mistaken the field and taken the wrong horse. She was really looking for one called Daisy Belle which used to pull a brewer's dray."

There came a pause, followed by a dry chuckle. "Grey Dawn's never seen a brewer's dray in her life! But she knows Epsom Downs like the back of her hand — if you take my meaning!"

Holly did, indeed, take his meaning. She felt sick with apprehension. "Will she be all right? Abigail, I mean."

"Oh, I should think so! As I said, she was sitting her remarkably well, although clearly unable to control the direction they were taking. My guess is they'll slow down when they reach Badger's Wood. That's where I've sent my agent in the Land-Rover, anyway. He'll soon sort them out. Might be an idea if someone came over, though. Girl could be in a state of shock."

"I'll come over right way," Holly assured him, "if you'll kindly tell me where you live."

"Two miles out of Marlingham on the London road. House stands back on the right. Turn off through a pair of iron gates and over a cattle-grid."

Holly was driving through the outskirts of Marlingham before she realised she must be on her way to the Manor that John had spoken of. So, it was Sir Henry Jarvis she'd been speaking to.

She found him — a plump, balding little man with a round, cherubic face and bushy side-whiskers — on the terrace in front of a picturesque Elizabethan mansion.

"Good of you to come! All's well, I gather. Johnson's just rung to say he's caught up with them and no damage done to either. He's giving them a breather, then riding Grey Dawn back himself and the girl's driving the Land-Rover."

"That's a relief! I'm really most awfully sorry," Holly added, beginning to feel guilty now that she knew Abbie was all right.

"Not quite the ride she'd planned, eh?"

"She'd only intended to ride Daisy around the field," Holly explained. "While she got to know her. Mr. Hawkins, the vet., had said we could use her to pull our cart."

The blue eyes twinkled at her mischievously. "Going in to the rag and bone business, are you?"

"No, bread actually!" said Holly calmly. "Delivered, freshly baked, to your door each morning."

"I thought that was a luxury that went out with steam trains and kippers," said Sir Henry. "Come in and have a glass of sherry and tell me all about it."

He led her from the terrace into a vast, panelled hall where Holly had a fleeting impression of a wide, stone staircase; of windows set high up above a minstrels' gallery; of huge, glass cabinets filled with china that would have been more at home in a museum.

"Come into the study," invited Sir Henry, turning down a side-passage. "Cosier!"

He was right. Compared with the grandiose gloom of the hall, the little room was a cluttered haven of domesticity. A coal fire burned before a shabby hearth-rug occupied by a large, marmalade cat. A set of sporting prints hung, lop-sidedly, above the mantlepiece, and a scuffed, leather armchair stood castor-deep in a wash of Sunday newspapers. Over all hung the pungent odour of cigar smoke.

"No woman's ever allowed in here," said Sir Henry complacently, adding quickly when Holly came to an abrupt halt, "I mean to tidy up! Now, where should you sit?"

It was a reasonable question to pose, for every chair held its own particular miscellany — books, tobacco-pouches, old copies of *Horse and Hound,* something that looked remarkably like several pairs of Sir Henry's old socks.

"This will do beautifully." Holly scooped up a fraying sweater from a little, velvet-covered chair, thus revealing a long-stemmed, cherry-wood pipe and a packet of ginger nuts.

"I wondered where that had got to!" Sir Henry pounced gleefully upon the pipe. "Now, some sherry." He crossed to a side-table holding decanters and glasses, then turned and gave Holly a careful scrutiny. "Dry, I think?"

Holly, wondering how on earth he'd reached that conclusion, told him that she did, indeed, prefer a dry sherry.

"Can always tell!" said Sir Henry in a gratified tone, and poured generous measures into a pair of engraved, crystal glasses. He handed one to Holly and took the other to the leather armchair. "Now," he settled himself comfortably, "tell me all about this bakery business of yours."

To her surprise it took Holly a good half-hour to cover everything, beginning with her astonished reaction to Great-aunt Gertrude's legacy, up until yesterday's meetings. For the most part, Sir Henry made no comment but listened intently, only occasionally asking for more information upon some point he was unsure of.

Holly, remembering John's remark that Sir Henry wasn't among those who were investing in the company, found herself glossing quickly over the way in which the enterprise was to be financed. It seemed enough that Abbie had run off with his horse, without seeming to suggest, however unintentionally, that he might like to part with his money. On the other hand, of course, it was probably more a case of the horse running off with Abbie!

She had just reached the end of her story, explaining once again how Abbie had intended making friends with Daisy

Belle that morning, when they heard sounds of her return. Sir Henry led the way out to the stable-yard. A somewhat pale-faced Abbie was getting out of a Land-Rover, and a large, grey horse was being led into a loose-box by a man whom Holly recognised as Mr. Johnson.

"I'm extremely sorry about my foolish mistake, Sir Henry . . ." Abbie began, but was immediately waved to silence by Sir Henry.

"Say no more about it! Might not have met two charming young ladies if you hadn't! Now, come along inside and warm yourself up."

But Abbie, once her apologies had been made, clearly wanted to get home as quickly as possible. And Holly was in agreement.

"Bath and bed," she said firmly. "And we'll collect your car later."

Just before they drove off Sir Henry bent his head to Holly's window. "I'll be in touch. You and your young man must come over to dinner."

"You certainly seem to have made a hit there," said Abbie as they crossed the cattle-grid.

"He probably doesn't realise I'll be back in London this evening," said Holly. What she did find a little strange was the way in which Sir Henry had included Brian in the invitation. She'd barely mentioned him in her telling of the bakehouse saga.

At least, Abbie's escapade gave everyone plenty to talk about when they got back to Marlingham. By the time Caroline had put her to bed and Holly had explained what had happened, any embarrassment she might have felt over seeing John again had gone. and yet she knew that the relationship between them had undergone a subtle change. It was unlikely, for instance, to be entirely concern for Abbie that made him seem so preoccupied and reserved. 'Aloof' was not a word she would normally have applied to such a friendly, outgoing man, but now she had the distinct impression that John was very definitely keeping her at a distance.

And that could mean only one thing; their brief intimacy, as far as he was concerned, had been a ghastly mistake, and was not, under any circumstances, to be repeated.

She tried to be philosophical about it. After all, she had already made a bargain with herself that she would take her cue from John's own behaviour; and it certainly made for lack of complications as far as Brian was concerned. Although she gave John an otherwise full account of her visit to the Manor, she made no mention of Sir Henry's invitation to dinner. It was unlikely, anyway, that anything would come of it.

But she was wrong. On the following evening the telephone in her flat rang. Holly, in the middle of preparing dinner for herself and Brian, handed him the potato-masher and went to answer it.

"Hope you'll forgive the liberty of using a telephone number you hadn't actually given me," came Sir Henry's voice, without preamble, "but you mentioned that you lived in London, so I looked you up. Still in the country myself and staying for the week. Would you be coming down on Friday? If so, wondered if you'd care to have dinner with me. I'm inviting your young man, too, of course."

"I'd love to," said Holly immediately. "Thank you. And my young man does just happen to be with me at the moment! Would you hold on, and I'll ask him now." Without waiting for a reply, she put down the receiver and went back to the kitchen.

"Brian, we've been asked out to dinner on Friday by a perfectly charming gentleman in Marlingham. Would you like to come?" He hadn't, she noticed, got very far with the potatoes.

"Can't manage Friday, sweetie. Nor can you. It's the rugger club dinner and dance."

"That's the first I've heard of it! I'm afraid I've already said yes to this invitation."

"Oh, come on, Holly! I always go to the rugger club do."

"Right!" she said crisply. "But I'm afraid you'll have to go without me."

"My young man had another engagement," she told Sir Henry, "but I'll be coming, of course."

"Matter of fact, my dear," he sounded faintly embarrassed, "I think we may have our wires crossed, as they say. I've already asked the young man *I* had in mind. Young Lorimer from the Book Shop."

"Oh, I see!" Holly suddenly began to giggle uncontrollably.

"Just as well your London young man said no, eh?" And Sir Henry chuckled his appreciation of what could have been a delicate situation.

Holly managed to control her giggles. "Just as well!" she agreed.

"See you about seven-thirty on Friday, then."

"Goodbye, Sir Henry, and thank you."

Turning to go back into the kitchen she found Brian leaning in the doorway and watching her curiously. "Did you say Sir Henry?"

117

"Yes, Sir Henry Jarvis. He lives at Marlingham Manor."

Brian whistled. "But he's chairman of Jarvis's Pharmaceutical Products. One of our most important clients. Why on earth didn't you tell me it was he who was inviting us to dinner? Ring him back straight away," he commanded, "and say that I'm free, after all."

"Too late, I'm afraid. He'll have asked someone else by now." Pointless to explain that he'd already done so anyway.

For a moment Brian considered her in silence, and then he said, "It's that fellow, Lorimer, isn't it?"

"Only because Sir Henry wants to know more about the bakery. He was the natural choice."

"No doubt!" said Brian caustically. But he wasn't, Holly saw to her relief as furious as he might have been. He seemed, in fact, to be more interested in Sir Henry than in John Lorimer. Grateful that his wrath had apparently been diverted, Holly gave him a humorous account of Abbie's escapade with Grey

Dawn and of how it had led to her meeting with Sir Henry. Encouraged by his obvious enjoyment of the tale, she went on to tell him about the plans for the bakery; after all, he seemed to be growing more amenable to her involvement in it.

With a classic gown of heavy white silk carefully folded into a suitcase she travelled down to Marlingham on the Friday afternoon.

Calling at the Book Shop to discover how they were getting to the Manor she found John alone in the shop rearranging some books on a shelf. He looked up and saw her standing in the doorway, and for a moment his face lit up with the familiar, welcoming smile. And then the smile faded abruptly. At least, the shape of it was still there, but it no longer reached his eyes. They had grown wary, almost cold, and Holly felt her heart plunge into despair.

Gone was the happy, light-hearted rapport, the striking of verbal sparks from each other so that conversation flowed, swift and scintillating. And all because gratitude and the intimacy of the moment had caught her off guard, had caused her to initiate a kiss that had seemed to encompass so much more than the simple placing of one mouth upon another. At the thought of it Holly felt her cheeks tingle with shame. For to John it had clearly meant only acute embarrassment. Holly lifted her chin, determined to match his coolness with her own.

"Whose driving who tonight?" she asked.

"Neither of us. Sir Henry, wishing us to enjoy his hospitality to the full, is sending his car. It will pick you up at seven and myself at five past."

And they would, she knew instinctively, sit as far away from each other as possible. Ridiculous to imagine that she wanted it otherwise.

8

WHILE she was dressing that evening, Holly discovered that she badly needed a full-length mirror. That would mean another trip to the Glory Hole. And, while she was there, she'd look out for some small dining-chairs — it would be nice to be able to return the Lorimer hospitality.

Wriggling into her dress, she noticed cobwebs festooning a corner of the ceiling and saw at the same time that the wall-paper was peeling. Hurriedly, she looked the other way. Decorating was something that would have to wait for a very long time.

When the lights of a car shone down the lane, she anxiously scanned her face in the little mirror over the bathroom washbasin and hoped that the rest of her looked all right. Could she possibly ask John to wait while she ran in and used Caroline's mirror?

But as soon as the car turned into the square, the door of the Book Shop opened and John ran down the steps. Just as she'd anticipated, he sat as far away from her as he could, and made little attempt at conversation, beyond asking if she was quite comfortable now at the cottage.

"Fine!" she said. "Although I think I must visit the Glory Hole again in the morning to buy a few more things."

"I see," he said, but made no suggestion that he should accompany her. The silence between them was almost tangible. Holly felt forced to break it.

"Did you know," she heard herself ask, "that Sir Henry said he was inviting my young man, and I thought he meant Brian?"

"Well, naturally!" he said stonily.

"Of course," she felt compelled to add, "I'm delighted that he meant you!"

"There's absolutely no need," he said tersely, "to make these wildly inaccurate statements on my account."

If he'd actually put out both hands

and pushed her away from him, Holly couldn't have felt more rejected.

"I didn't . . . " she began miserably. But then they were on the gravel sweep in front of the Manor, and Sir Henry's butler had appeared in the open doorway.

"We seem," said John Lorimer in a tone of relief "to have arrived."

Holly said no more.

The butler showed them into a drawing-room opening off the hall that Holly had crossed on her previous visit. As Sir Henry came forward to greet them, Holly saw that a chair was already occupied by an attractive woman, probably a few years older than herself. Her thick, dark hair was drawn back into a knot at the nape of her neck, in a style that suited to perfection the classic symmetry of her features; a short, straight nose above a delectably curving mouth, dark eyes, deep-set and intelligent. A person, Holly decided, of great charm and culture.

"Think you already know Miss Olivia Harding, Lorimer," said Sir Henry, making the introductions.

"Miss Harding's my neighbour," he explained to Holly. "Her land runs with mine."

"By that he means my cottage stands at the end of his park!" said Olivia Harding in a rich vibrant voice, stretching out a hand to Holly. Her grip was cool and firm.

Nice, as well as beautiful, thought Holly, and wasn't in the least surprised when John, with obvious sincerity, said, "Livvy, it *is* good to see you! It's been far too long!"

"I've been abroad a lot lately," she said.

"Any interesting finds?"

Olivia shrugged. "Nothing very spectacular. One or two things that might be worth a little when I've had them restored."

"She's being very secretive," Sir Henry complained. "Olivia's a collector of beautiful objects," he explained to Holly. "Asked her — no, implored her — to keep an eye open for some genuine Birmingham horse brasses for me, and she won't tell me if she's found any or not. Horsewhip her, if I had my way!" His friendly grin belied the ferocity of his words.

"I've told you, Henry," Olivia said, "I'm not raising your hopes until I'm quite sure. I've heard of someone who may have a set, but I want to have a good look at them first. But, don't worry. You'll get your brasses in the end. As you get most things you want!"

"Not the only one! This little lady," he nodded towards Holly, now ensconced, glass in hand, in a deep armchair beside the fire, "is as determined as they come. Doesn't look it, but she is. Tell Olivia all about the good home-cooking you've got in store for us, my dear."

Holly shrivelled with embarrassment. However kind his intentions, their amiable host was making her feel like an apple-cheeked, country girl beside this glamorous, artistic creature. And where could she begin, anyway? She looked despairingly at John.

"I'm afraid I'm the determined one

in this case," he said smoothly. "Holly has as much idea of running a bakery as I have a fashion show, which is her particular line."

Blessing him for his tact, Holly gave him a grateful smile. "But I'm growing as keen as John about preserving our country heritage," she said.

"Tell me more," pleaded Olivia Harding. "You can't imagine how I yearn for a really crisp roll or croissant with my breakfast coffee."

"There you are, my dear," said a delighted Sir Henry to Holly. "One more regular customer for you. Livvy, how many rolls can you manage a day? Half a dozen?"

She rolled her eyes to the ceiling. "Have you *no* regard for my figure? But tell me more about this venture, John. It sounds something close to my own heart."

It wasn't only 'things' that were close to her heart, Holly decided, watching carefully. There was room for people, too. And John Lorimer could easily be one of them. There was a calm possessiveness about the way she looked at him; the oh-so-casual hand that fell, quite naturally, on to his arm — and stayed there. And clearly, he was basking in the radiant smile, the infectious chuckle, the cleverly turned phrase.

It was impossible to say exactly when it happened, but what had started as a conversational foursome had become two separate entities, with Sir Henry discussing the finer points of country life with Holly, and the other two moving with lightning swiftness from one subject to another; from bakeries and bread to books and paintings and then, by way of the art galleries of Rome and Florence, to the Italian holiday Olivia had taken last summer, and the Spanish one she was planning for next. Holly knew, because she was finding it extremely difficult to concentrate upon what Sir Henry was saying.

The remainder of the evening followed the same pattern. Although, now and then, Olivia chatted politely with Holly and found, in fact, that they shared several mutual acquaintances in the fashion world, eventually she would turn back to John and the quick, conversational interplay would be resumed. She's the perfect foil for him, thought Holly wistfully, and wondered why the sight of John Lorimer enjoying himself so hugely with another woman should cause her so much pain.

"Don't you agree with me, my dear?" enquired Sir Henry in her ear.

"Er — absolutely!" said Holly abstractedly.

"Knew you would! So, it's coffee in the drawing-room then, Pearson," said Sir Henry to his butler.

Really! thought Holly, I must pull myself together; and, for the rest of the evening, was an admirable guest, listening attentively to the stories told by her host in between making her own contribution to the conversation. But when the time came for them to leave she found that she felt ridiculously tired, as if the effort she had put into enjoying herself had exhausted her out of all proportion to the result.

Olivia, living so near, said that she would walk home, but Sir Henry insisted that the car should take her, so all three guests left together.

"Keep me posted," said Sir Henry to Holly as he stood on the steps, "and don't forget to bring that London young man of yours to see me. Goodnight, Lorimer, you must invite us all to breakfast when the bakery goes into action. Goodnight, Livvy, I'll be in to see you before too long."

They dropped Olivia beside an old-world cottage where moonlit lawns lapped rockeries and rose-beds, and Holly found herself thinking guiltily of the garden of Rosemary Cottage. Tomorrow, perhaps, she'd find time to start digging.

"A charming person!" Holly heard herself remark as they drove on.

"Very!" said John dismissively, as if Olivia's charm was none of her business. And then he changed the subject. "You know, I think we should do more than just invite Sir Henry to breakfast when we open. Why don't we ask him to perform the opening ceremony?"

"As long as he doesn't think it's a roundabout way of asking for his money," said Holly. "He hasn't offered to invest in the bakery, has he?"

"No, I think he assumes that we have enough investors already. And now that we've enjoyed his hospitality I'd be loathe to suggest it. But his patronage should count for a great deal."

And for the remainder of the short journey they discussed Sir Henry's rôle at the opening. "We might get Olivia to come, too," said John thoughtfully. "She'd lend a touch of glamour to any occasion."

"I can imagine!" said Holly, and hoped that she didn't sound as two-faced as she felt.

Next morning Abbie came round soon after nine.

"John tells me you want some furniture, and there does just happen to be an auction at the Old Rectory this morning. I've brought some sandwiches, in case it goes on a bit, but I thought we ought to get there early so that we can have a good look-round before the sale starts. I just hope there won't be too many dealers."

"Do you happen to know one called Olivia Harding?" Holly asked, hastily piling up her breakfast dishes, then following Abbie out to her car.

"Of course! Charm the birds off the trees, would our Livvie! But not — so far — my Uncle John. Although it's not from lack of trying."

"I think," said Holly lightly, "that he might be weakening!" And she gave Abbie a brief account of the previous evening.

"Well," Abbie conceded, "she's certainly stunning to look at. But Mum thinks she's rather too high-powered for John."

Holly, for no reason at all, suddenly noticed that it was a perfect autumn day. The early mist had disappeared and fields of stubble were shining like freshly minted gold under a mellow sun.

Hedges, thickly berried with rose-hips and hawthorn, were brilliant against the pale-blue sky. And Caroline, she reminded herself was a person of excellent good sense!

At first sight the sale seemed to contain only an uninspiring collection of well-worn, family cast-offs. Bundles of walking-sticks, umbrellas and butterfly-nets leaned precariously against hat-stands and old-fashioned fire-guards; sagging armchairs held dusty pictures and distorted mirrors. But here and there, among the bric-à-brac, were several lovely pieces.

"Just look at that chest!" said Abbie suddenly. "Have you ever seen anything so beautiful?"

It was of dark oak, its lid shining with a patina acquired from years of constant polishing, its panelled sides carved with an intricate design of flowers and leaves.

"And look," said Holly, her finger tracing the shape, "here's a tiny squirrel with a nut between its paws!" And then she noticed a portly robin peeping coyly through fronds of fern. The panel was, in fact, alive with animals and birds.

"The man who carved this," said Holly reverently, "must have loved the countryside. Oh, Abbie, I'd give anything to have it for the cottage."

"In that case," said the resourceful Abbie, "we'll sit on it until the sale begins! That way, we might manage to keep it to ourselves." And she immediately sat herself down upon the chest, spreading her coat as widely as possible.

"You're forgetting that yesterday was probably a preview day," said Holly. "All the dealers will be after it." But, nevertheless, she joined Abbie on the chest.

They were, of course, prised off it on several occasions, but Abbie had soon perfected a neat line of patter. "So sorry! Are we in your way?" but still sitting there, hindering any closer inspection. "Of course," to Holly, "woodworm's always a problem in anything as old as this!"

"Abbie, how can you?" Holly remonstrated through her giggles, after the ruse had succeeded for the second time.

"All in a good cause!" said Abbie. "And I'm not actually *saying* there's woodworm in it. If they want to assume there is, that's up to them. Anyway, let's start eating our sandwiches now!" And soon, all the paraphernalia of a regular picnic was spread out over the chest.

They stayed there until the sale had begun and the auctioneer and his entourage were upon them.

"And what have we here?" asked the auctioneer, a genial young man with an entertaining line in patter. "Lot 76. One carved oak chest and two attractive young ladies to go with it!" He winked at Abbie and she winked back. "What am I bid?"

There were a couple of ribald remarks and then, to Holly's bitter disappointment, the bidding started in earnest between two poker-faced men who had clearly already assessed its value. Up went the price until it had almost reached the limit Holly had set herself. Then one dealer suddenly dropped out of the bidding. The auctioneer cast a speculative eye over the crowd.

"Any other offers? Going, then at . . .

"Guineas!" Holly heard her own voice say desperately.

"Attagirl!" breathed Abbie.

The dealer turned and gave her an appraising stare; and then, deciding apparently that he had nothing to worry about, nodded again at the auctioneer.

"Another ten, I'm bid!" said the auctioneer, presumably able to interpret exactly the wishes of the poker-faced man.

"That chest," suddenly said an old gentleman in the crowd, speaking in a very clear, light-pitched voice, "was carved by my great-great-grandfather. It should stay in Marlingham where it's always been. You have it, miss," he said to Holly, as if it was his to give. "You're going to start up the old bakery, I hear."

News travelled fast in Marlingham!

135

Holly found herself nodding at the auctioneer to the manner born. There came a little burst of hand-clapping and cheering from the crowd.

The auctioneer looked at the dealer, and the cheering immediately turned to booing, almost as if they were daring him to bid again. The auctioneer quickly called the crowd to order, but the dealer's poise had slipped. Casting swift, almost furtive glances around him he was clearly in two minds whether to continue the bidding. The auctioneer took the matter into his own hands.

"Do I take it you've withdrawn, sir?"

The dealer nodded and immersed himself quickly in his catalogue.

"Next item?" enquired the auctioneer, turning to his clerk, but not before he'd given Holly an approving smile.

"Oh, thank you!" said Holly to the room at large, and the old man and the auctioneer in particular, and the next minute Abbie was hugging her with unrestrained glee.

"How," Holly suddenly wondered as

the crowd moved on with the auctioneer, "are we going to get it home? Do you know anyone . . . " And then stopped abruptly and stared at Abbie.

"What's the matter? Don't you want it after all? Or have I got a genuine antique spider in my hair?"

"Neither! I was just realising I'd called Rosemary Cottage, home!"

"Just as well! A chest like this needs a good one! You can't just pop it down any old where."

"You're right," said Holly slowly. "I've really burned my boats now."

"How about a working weekend then? Before you change your mind. Mike will collect the chest in his Land-Rover and then we'll get organised with paint-brushes."

"That means we'll have to decide on colour schemes. And some of the walls need plastering."

"John can do that. He loves wielding a trowel."

"If he's free," said Holly quickly, suddenly remembering Olivia Harding.

"Stop being difficult," said Abbie. "He must be free!"

And he was. Pausing only briefly when they'd tracked him down in the shop, before nodding his agreement, he said, "And don't go buying paint before you see what I've got in my workshop. We had plenty left over from the last time I painted this place."

"If you're sure," said Holly gratefully.

"And what," he asked equably, "has brought on this sudden burst of domesticity?"

Abbie answered for her. "It's this magnificent chest we've just bought at the rectory sale. It's brought out all her nesting instincts."

"Delighted to hear it." He glanced quizzically at Holly. "And d'you think your fiancé will share your enthusiasm?"

That same thought had been troubling Holly for the last hour, but Abbie put a hand on her arm and shook a reproving finger at her uncle.

"Stop trying to confuse the issue! When he sees what a marvellous job we're going to make of Rosemary Cottage he won't even consider living anywhere else! Now I wonder," she added thoughtfully, "what Mike thought he was going to be doing this afternoon?"

By that evening Rosemary Cottage was a different place. Fresh curtains billowed at all the windows — blue and white checked gingham in the kitchen, rosy chintz in the living-room, sprigged cotton in the bedrooms, and what John swore was a favourite towelling shirt of his in the bathroom! As a means of getting back on to the old, familiar footing with him, Holly couldn't have chosen a more favourable method if she'd tried. With people around him, he seemed able to relax and there was certainly no shortage of people! Not only had Abbie co-opted her mother and Mike, he in turn had brought along a couple of his friends.

"Building the pyramids," Abbie said extravagantly to Holly, as they paused on the tiny lawn after delivering cups of tea to the workers, "must have been like this!"

Mike, looking down from the trestle placed between two step-ladders from which he and John were carefully pointing the old bricks, said, "Well, we're not exactly stripped to the waist, beavering away in the hot sun, but I do see what you mean."

Holly could, too. Caroline was in the bay of the sitting-room window, head bent industriously over her sewing-machine; clearly visible through the open front door, Mike's two friends were painting the tiny hall a delicate, egg-shell blue and, up on the roof the thatcher — not really due until the following weekend, but persuaded by Abbie that he could easily start today was weaving lengths of golden reed into the weaker parts of the thatch.

"It's very kind of everyone," said Holly.

"Our pleasure!" Mike assured her, "and, as far as I'm concerned, there'll be plenty of opportunity to repay in

140

kind. I'm always wanting someone to nurse a sick sheep or sit on a bull's head for me!"

"Pay no attention!" said Abbie. "Country vets. are notorious for trying to lead the local females astray."

"Only one of them!" said Mike. "Which leads me to suggest that the four of us go out for dinner tonight. How about it, John?"

But John seemed to be giving his undivided attention to a hair-line crack in one of the bricks. "Sorry!" he said. "I'm afraid I'm already booked."

"You don't usually go out on a Saturday night," said Abbie indignantly.

"Since when," asked her uncle caustically, "have you been responsible for my social calendar? Anyway, it's business as much as pleasure. Olivia Harding wants my professional opinion on some ancient books she's acquired."

"Can't you tell her your working hours are strictly nine till five?" asked Abbie wickedly.

"In that case," John made a play of

141

glancing at his watch, "you'll excuse me if I get on with the job in hand! The front door needs new hinges and Holly will want to lock it tonight."

"And we've got to decide on a colour-scheme for the kitchen," Holly reminded Abbie.

"I thought we'd agreed on primrose and white," said Abbie, but she allowed herself to be led away.

In fact it was nearly seven o'clock before people put down their tools. Once dusk had fallen, and the outside work had been left for the day, everyone had combined on a massive operation indoors. Except for freshly plastered walls in the kitchen and bathroom, the rooms had all received a fresh wash of colour. "And we'll do the bedrooms tomorrow," John promised.

Holly still didn't possess a full-length mirror, but the carved chest, after being tried in several places, had finally come to rest under the sitting-room window, and now, holding a vase of copper-beech leaves preserved by Caroline, looked as if it had been there all its life.

"The smell of paint may upset you," Caroline said to Holly. "Why not sleep with us tonight?"

But Holly found that she couldn't bear to leave Rosemary Cottage in all its fresh, new beauty.

"Well, come and keep me company over dinner, anyway. Abbie and Mike are going out, and even John's deserting me."

"Why not eat here with me?" Holly suggested. "If bacon and eggs are all right. And I've a bottle of wine I brought down from London, especially for the occasion."

She saw John's head come up, at that, and for a moment she thought he was going to ask if he could stay as well. But he only looked down again at the brushes he was cleaning at the kitchen sink. Olivia Harding, naturally, would have first claim upon his company.

9

ONLY ten days remained before the opening of the bakery, and Holly had agreed to spend the following weekend at Marlingham to help with the final plans. To her pleased surprise Brian seemed quite content with this arrangement.

"I might even be able to get down myself on the Sunday. How about my driving down for lunch? Then afterwards we could drop in on Sir Henry. You said he'd like to meet me."

Privately Holly thought that the invitation had only been extended on a very casual basis, but she didn't demur. Brian's sudden interest in Marlingham was not to be discouraged at any price. She would telephone Sir Henry on Sunday morning to make sure that it was convenient.

"I'm not yet organised enough to hold

a lunch-party at the cottage," she told Caroline, John and Abbie when she called on them on Saturday morning, "but why don't we all go out for a meal tomorrow? Brian's coming down."

She hadn't intended to make the occasion sound so important, but John raised his eyebrows. "And you want to make sure the natives are polite! Perhaps it's just as well I won't be available."

"Mike and I will be," said Abbie firmly.

"You seem to be very conversant with that young man's movements, all of a sudden," her mother observed.

Abigail helped herself to a handful of currants from the heap Caroline was mixing into a cake. "Yes, I do, don't I?" she agreed non-committally. "Bags I lick the bowl when you've finished!"

"I can't think who else you imagine is going to crave such a juvenile privilege!" said John dryly. "I'm sure Holly doesn't."

She was probably being over-sensitive in imagining a note of criticism in even that trivial statement. "By the way," she said lightly, "my editor's off to New York two days before the opening, so I won't be able to come down until after she's gone."

"Don't worry," said Caroline, "we seem to be fairly well organised. Everything except the rolls will be made the day before. Bread for sandwiches; cakes and pies. I'm making the pie fillings up here, and Abbie will help Mrs. Baxter bake them. We shall manage perfectly."

"And how are you spending the rest of today?" Abbie asked Holly.

"Now that the plaster's dry I'll finish painting the bathroom and kitchen," said Holly.

"Let's hope you get Brian's approval tomorrow," said Abbie. "It would be super if you decided to live here after you're married."

Out of the corner of her eye, Holly saw John turn away as if no longer interested in the discussion.

"I'll be down later to see if I can help," Abbie continued. Silly to feel so hurt that John didn't offer as well.

In fact Brian was surprisingly enthusiastic when he arrived next day. "I've never seen such a change in a place!" He wandered from one freshly painted room to the next. "Still needs some basic alterations, of course. A bigger bathroom, more room in the kitchen."

To Holly, the proportions seemed just right, but she had no wish to argue. "So, you wouldn't mind living here after all?" she asked.

"Well, I wouldn't go quite as far as that! But it would certainly make a splendid week-end retreat if we could afford it. Just the sort of place to invite a client if you wanted to talk business in a pleasant, relaxed atmosphere."

Holly let that pass without comment. She wasn't at all sure that she wanted Rosemary Cottage used as a retreat for weary business men.

"I haven't mentioned it to you before," continued Brian expansively, "but things are looking up for me at the agency. Alan Medlicott's going to another firm and I'm first in line for his job. That's why

I thought it might be useful if we could call in on Sir Henry this afternoon."

Holly stared at him. "I don't understand the connection."

Brian gave her a maddeningly paternal smile. "Surely I mentioned that Jarvis Pharmaceuticals is a client of ours. One of Medlicott's babies. If I can get Sir Henry to put a word in for me with the old man, it would help no end."

To Holly the idea was completely repugnant. "Brian, I couldn't possibly take you to see Sir Henry with such an idea in mind."

"Come off it, pet! Don't tell me you and Lorimer didn't wangle an invitation to dinner with him for the express purpose of raising money for the bakery."

"Certainly not! Sir Henry isn't putting a penny into it, and John only said on the way home the other night that he wouldn't dream of asking him after we'd been his guests."

"Then it's obvious Lorimer hasn't a clue about business methods. Pity help your bakcry, that's all I can say." But *that* apparently, *wasn't* all. "So Lorimer drove you home afterwards, did he? Just the two of you? Very cosy! And you asked him in for a nightcap, no doubt?"

"You're completely wrong — in every respect. Sir Henry's chauffeur drove us home. And dropped John first. Anyway," she added conclusively, "he has a girl friend. A most attractive woman who was also at the Manor that evening."

"Do I detect a note of regret?"

"I hate you when you say things like that! Let me go, please! You're hurting!" His hands were holding her upper arms, the fingers pressing deep into the flesh.

"Hate me, do you? I think you've got it wrong, my pet. You want me as much as I want you, and you know it! Anyway, you deserve better than a village Romeo, yearning for his lost youth."

His lips were upon hers, his hands moving to pull her body against his, her head forced backwards by the roughness of his kiss. She wrenched her mouth away.

"Brian! Please stop!"

149

"Funny! You never used to mind!"

And he was right, of course. Once her own body would have quickened to his. But now, passion wasn't enough. She wanted gentleness, consideration — love. As if he sensed her change of mood, he took his mouth from hers and began pressing quick, teasing kisses over her face and neck.

"Holly, you've kept me waiting too long!" But it was no good. Brian, whether fiercely possessive or gentle and persuasive, no longer had the power to move her. She moved away from him.

"Brian, I'm sorry!"

"I'm sorry, too, pet! I mustn't rush you."

Suddenly, he looked so humble and contrite she was moved to pity, and made the only suggestion she could think of to cheer him up. "I'll ring Sir Henry," she promised. "See if we can call in on him after we've had lunch. But, Brian, *please* don't ask him anything about business. It would really upset me if he thought

I'd only taken you for that reason."

He cheered up immediately. "Good girl! But where will you ring from?" The bakery telephone wasn't to be installed until the following week.

"I'll ask if I can do it from the Book Shop. I said we'd pick Abbie and Mike up at twelve-thirty. We're lunching at the local pub."

But, in fact, the telephone call to Sir Henry was never made.

"He's not there this weekend," John told them. "When I rang to ask if he'd consider opening the bakery for us, he mentioned he was staying in town."

"You mean he's actually going to open it?" Brian's astonishment had overcome the distinct coolness with which he'd been treating John.

"Wouldn't miss it for the world, I gather! Apparently," John turned to Holly, "he'd been hoping we'd ask him ever since he heard about it."

"I suppose you realise how fortunate you are," said Brian. "He's one of the most sought-after tycoons in industry."

"I had heard," said John quietly.

Brian turned to Holly. "When did you say the opening was, darling?" She told him. "Bother! I'm away for practically the whole week. Otherwise I wouldn't have minded coming down myself." He thought for a moment. "You know, it's probably as well we can't see him this afternoon, Holly. You would have been an inhibiting influence. I'll call sometime, on my own."

"You know Sir Henry?" John asked.

"Not yet!" said the other cheerfully. "But I'm hoping to handle his next advertising campaign. So, it's a question of no stone unturned! Like me to have a word with him on your behalf? Get him to invest a few thousand in the bakery?"

Heavens! thought Holly. John will probably hit him for that! And I can't say I'd blame him. And, in fact, John's mouth had tightened to a thin, white line, his eyes like steel.

"I think I can manage my own business affairs, thank you."

"Here come Abbie and Mike," said

Holly gratefully. "Perhaps we'll see you later, John?"

"I doubt it!" And if he'd actually added, 'Not if I can help it!' his meaning couldn't have been more clear.

It was ironic, she thought, that now Brian was showing such an interest in the bakery she wished devoutly that he would not!

In spite of everything, lunch was an enjoyable meal. Abbie and Mike, obviously happy to be in each other's company, were easy to be with, and Brian was at his most attentive, just as he'd been when they'd first met. It was strange how the coming of Rosemary Cottage into her life seemed to have changed all her values.

Over coffee, the talk turned, naturally, to the opening of the bakery. "I've arranged for Mary Edwards from the Gift Shop," Abbie explained, "to run the café for me while I'm out on deliveries."

"I take it," said Brian a trifle pompously, "that you're running an advance publicity campaign?"

"Of course!" said Abbie airily. "I've told all my tea-shop customers, and they've told all their friends. And John's told all *his* customers. And Mike's told every cat and dog for miles around!"

"Not forgetting," said Mike solemnly, "all the carrier pigeons I've given messages to!"

"Believe me . . . " Brian began.

"Not to worry!" said Abigail. "We're only pulling your leg. There are posters all over town, and every household in the neighbourhood has received a beautifully printed leaflet specially designed by me. And John will tour the town with a loudspeaker van the day before the opening."

"Oh," said Brian, slightly mollified, "I see! Well, I just hope the coverage has been adequate, that's all."

"In the absence of any offers from the leading advertising agencies," said Abbie wickedly, "we were thrown on to our own resources."

"And believe me," said Mike fondly, "Abbie's resources would put even your

154

agency to shame!"

But Brian was in no mood for pleasantries. "If only I'd realised," he said sadly, "what an important event it was going to be."

And that Sir Henry Jarvis would be opening it! thought Holly. But wisely held her peace. "I suppose the invitations have been sent out?" she asked Abigail.

"Well, there's open-house for everyone, but special people like our financiers, Livvie Harding and that notorious veterinary surgeon, Mike Hawkins, have received personal invitations." Holly was grateful for the laughter that the remark provoked. So, Olivia was already classed as a 'special person' was she?

Some hours later Brian kissed Holly goodnight at the door of her flat. "Early night tonight, poppett. My flight to Düseldorf leaves at dawn."

She hoped her relief wasn't too obvious. "I'll phone you when I'm back," he promised.

10

HOLLY spent the next few days in a rush of hectic activity. Once her editor, Jill Colville, had left for the States life would be much easier. But meanwhile there were last-minute details to be arranged with the New York fashion houses, agreements to be reached about the release of information to the press, discussions with other editorial staff on the magazine, contingency plans to be drawn up in case expected copy shouldn't be forthcoming.

It was with a profound sense of relief that Holly eventually saw off the jumbo jet that had Jill on board, then went back to the office to clear up the debris.

"There's been an urgent call for you," said the girl who'd been taking care of her telephone, "from a Mr. Lorimer. He'll ring again in" she consulted her watch "one minute!"

Even as she finished speaking the phone was ringing.

"Holly? Sorry to be so precipitate! But I thought I ought to let you know what's happened."

"What?" Did ovens blow up? Pumps run dry? Flour go mouldy?

"It's the Baxters. They're going to be all right in a week or two, the doctors say, but at the moment they're both tucked up in hospital suffering from shock and minor injuries. A friend was giving them a lift in his car and had the misfortune to skid on a greasy road and hit a tree. No-one's badly hurt, but we're on our own as far as the bakery is concerned, I'm afraid. If it had happened a week ago I would definitely have postponed the opening, but as things are I think we're past the point of no return. Everyone thinks it's the day after tomorrow and there simply isn't time to let them all know. So half of them would turn up to a non-event and we'd lose face for not sticking to our word. And that could be fatal. Abbie and Caroline are dead against postponing it. What do you think?"

Holly didn't hesitate. "I told you once I wouldn't know what to do with a packet of bread-mix, but I can pick up most things if I have to. Let's go ahead!"

"That's what I hoped you'd say! How soon can you get away?"

"Give me a couple of hours to settle things up here," said Holly, "and I'll be down this evening."

"Bless you!" said John Lorimer with feeling. "We'll be seeing you, then."

In spite of the difficulties that were bound to lie ahead, Holly felt a delicious tingle of anticipation. At least she and John seemed to be friends again.

"Just put them down there, Holly. Thanks!"

Abbie, the sleeves of her white overall rolled above her elbows, turned from the mound of foil pie-cases she was laying out on the work-top and nodded towards a vacant corner. Holly carefully put down her two heavy, metal canisters.

"Chicken and mushroom filling in this

one and steak and kidney in that. And your mother says, how about beef and onion?"

"If she's got the time and doesn't mind doing the onions, the more variety the better."

"I'll do the onions."

"How about a cup of tea before you start? You seem to have been saying 'I'll do this' and 'I'll do that' ever since you got here last night."

"Super. I'll make it."

"There she goes again! The girl thinks she's indispensable! Buckie made it before he went out to crawl under his van for the hundredth time."

"I thought I recognised his feet! Is it going to be all right for tomorrow?"

"It's very inconveniently choked its carburettor, he says. But it should be all right by tomorrow. Personally, I shall feel safer with Daisy Belle. Pour me one while you're there, would you? This is thirsty work."

Holly poured strong tea into thick mugs, and then sank gratefully down upon a bench. "When I woke up this morning I thought I must have left the fire on all night. The whole cottage was warm as toast, and there was this lovely smell drifting everywhere."

"I'm sure Albert will be glad to hear he's attending to your creature comforts, as well as baking the bread! He had the oven going all day yesterday to get the bricks warmed up."

"Where is he now?"

"Dashed home for a quick breakfast. He and John will be back to take the bread out of the oven in about fifteen minutes, and then I can put my pies in. The cakes will go in last of all."

"How did John make out as an apprentice baker?"

"I think Albert's quite proud of him. 'Think of the dough as your own worst enemy,' I heard him say, 'and punch like the devil!' They've used the mixers for most of it, this morning, but Albert couldn't resist mixing some dough by hand last night, and you know my uncle had to have a go, of course.

Let's hope he still feels as energetic this time next week."

"Of course I shall!" John had come through the door, an enormous woollen scarf draped over his old tweed jacket and his cheeks glowing with the cold. "I can't wait to see how my first loaves look. Where's Albert?"

"Let the poor man have his breakfast, for heaven's sake!" said Abbie. "Anyway, it's not time yet. Help yourself to tea!"

"I'll pour it," said Holly, getting up.

"I just hope," said Abbie darkly, "that all this energy will last out."

John grinned at Holly — the old, familiar grin that had come to mean so much to her.

She smiled back, and suddenly their eyes held and Holly's heart began to race. A tell-tale blush rose in her cheeks and she lowered her gaze, grateful that Abbie had her head bent over the mixture she was now spooning into the pastry-cases.

"I hope you both feel the same when you've been at it for a week or two," she said.

"The doctors hope that the Baxters will be back in about a fortnight," said John, "although they'll obviously have to take things easy for a while. I saw them last night and they're so cross to be missing all this. Holly, how long will you be able to stay with us?"

Holly forced her gaze upward and, to her relief, found that John was now looking at her with his customary friendly gaze.

"Jill should be away for at least a month. I've arranged for mail to be sent on to me here, and provided I can get up to the office about once a week I should be able to cope."

"That's fine! I've got someone working in the Book Shop for me, and Abbie's friend from the Gift Shop is running the café. It's important we keep that going because it could turn out to be an important outlet for the bakery."

"You mean a confectioner's shop in town?" Holly asked.

"Exactly. It would mean enlarging the premises, of course, but there'll be quite a few people who won't want to tie themselves down to a regular delivery each day but would like the opportunity of buying a fresh loaf when they want one. We could sell it from here, but the square is a much more central point."

"There!" said Abbie proudly. "My first batch of pies ready for when you take your loaves out, John. Now, I'll just pop out and take Daisy Belle her oats. I'm building her up for tomorrow."

"Would you like me to put your pies in?" Holly asked wistfully. From being a cold, empty extension of Rosemary Cottage, the bakehouse had now become a warm, fragrant power-house of activity, and she wanted, quite desperately, to be a part of it.

"Good idea!" said John quickly before Abbie could raise any objections. "I'll give you a hand."

"All right," said Abbie, "but make sure you check the time you put them in."

Her uncle pulled an imaginary forelock, and Abbie made a face at him while she shrugged into her duffel coat, yanked up the hood, and went out into the lane. Holly, suddenly self-conscious at finding herself alone with John, said the first thing that came into her head.

"You were quite right about the bakehouse warming the cottage. It was heavenly to wake up to this morning."

"Well, I'm glad something good for you is coming out of all this."

"But it's all good," she said, astonishment overcoming her embarrassment.

"Holly, are you sure I haven't landed you into something you're regretting? Making you come down here at a moment's notice to perform all sorts of menial tasks?"

"But I love doing them, feeling part of it all. And you didn't make me come — I volunteered."

"What did Brian have to say about it?"

"He wasn't there to ask. Anyway, he seems quite resigned to my keeping on the cottage and the bakery, now." It wasn't necessary to mention the proximity of Sir

Henry Jarvis as the major reason for his change of heart.

"D'you think you might even settle down here, eventually?"

"Well, I wouldn't go quite as far as that!" How could she explain her disinclination to live anywhere, married or not, where she would have to face him in the constant company of a beautiful creature like Olivia Harding, and even, perhaps, see him marry her?

"How's Olivia?" she asked. "I thought her such an attractive person when I met her the other evening." Extraordinary, this sadistic urge to rub salt into her self-inflicted wounds!

"Livvy? Yes, she's certainly that!" His face lost its preoccupation as he thought of Olivia, and he smiled reminiscently. "She's coming to the opening tomorrow."

"Super!" said Holly mechanically, suddenly feeling a surprising chill creep into the warmth of the bakery. But it could have been Albert, breezing in through the door like a man half his age, and already taking off his coat.

Buckie was on his heels.

"Bread's ready to come out in two minutes," announced Albert. "Buckie'll give us a hand, won't you, Buckie? When he's washed them, that is!"

Everyone laughed, including Buckie as he went out to the sink in the little wash-room.

"Van all right, now?" John asked.

"Yes, she'll do now," said Buckie.

They all watched in reverent silence while Albert opened the oven door, letting out a blast of hot air fragrant with the scent of newly baked bread, and peered solemnly inside. "Done to a turn," he said, taking the long, wooden peel handed him by Buckie and thrusting it into the oven. A moment later, he drew it out bearing tins from which the crusts of the loaves rose, crisp and golden. Soon, the tables near the oven were laden.

"You haven't got mine out yet," said John, peering anxiously over Albert's shoulder.

"Like to get them out yourself?" suggested Albert, handing over the peel.

John plunged it into the oven. A good minute later he brought it out again, with just one tin balanced — and precariously at that — on the end. Albert allowed himself a wicked chuckle.

"Not as easy as it looks," he said complacently.

At the next attempt John managed two, but one of these was burned almost black on one side.

"Good grief! How on earth did that happen?"

"Bit too near the flues," said Albert. "But don't worry. Plenty of people ask for it, just like that."

"Now for Abbie's pies," said John when the oven was empty. "Holly's going to help me put them in."

Carefully they placed the pies in the oven and firmly closed the door. Mindful of Abbie's instructions, Holly made a note of the time on a piece of paper and put it where Abbie would easily see it.

"What's your next job?" John enquired.

"Well, when this bread's cooled sufficiently I'm helping Caroline make hundreds of sandwiches. In the meantime I've got to collect cups for tomorrow's coffee from Abbie's café and borrow some more from the Royal Oak. Then there are the urns. We'd decided to have one in here and one in the cottage. I just hope we haven't catered for too many."

"I don't think so. Apart from a few people who may be ill or have pressing business elsewhere, Marlingham will turn out to a man. Not to mention children. School breaks for lunch at twelve, so if they hurry they'll just make it for Sir Henry's opening speech at twelve-fifteen. Since there'll be no-one at home to get their dinners they might just as well. Come on, I'll help you carry the cups. When will you want me again, Albert?"

"This afternoon, if you please. With all these buns for the morning, we'll need to make an early start."

"In that case I'll put the finishing touches to Daisy Belle's van. It's going to look rather spectacular for its inaugural run tomorrow. And then I must go and collect my loudspeaker car and remind Marlingham what's in store for them tomorrow. Coming, Holly?"

That night Holly crawled into the sleeping-bag that, at the moment, was so much more convenient than sheets and blankets, and decided that it had been an exhausting but satisfying day. Everything was ready for tomorrow, and the rapport between herself and John was as spontaneous as it used to be. The future, she decided sleepily, could look after itself. The present was quite perfect.

11

I T was, everyone agreed later, a highly successful opening. Even the things that went wrong actually added to its success.

Sir Henry's car, for instance, broke down. His chauffeur rang the bakery only minutes before he was due to arrive to explain that he was standing, at that very moment, on the roadside, half-way to Marlingham, trying to thumb a lift.

"I'll come over for him," John offered.

"Too late!" said the chauffeur grimly. "He's just stepped into an ice-cream van!"

"Should be another fifteen minutes, then," said John hopefully "Those things don't travel fast." It was a period of time that could be filled very usefully at the bakery. He himself had dropped a whole tray of buns that morning, and more had had to be baked; Daisy Belle, full of oats,

170

had refused for the first time in living memory, to be caught, and Abbie had fallen flat on her face in her efforts before calling Mike in to help. Holly, cocooned in scented warmth, had slept through her alarm.

"Do I look all right?" she asked breathlessly when Caroline arrived at the cottage.

"As pretty as ever!" Caroline assured her. "Here, let me do up that zip for you!"

"Thanks! Sure I'm not too dressy?" Her simply cut overdress was in dark brown wool, through which ran a fine strand of gold thread; the matching polo-necked blouse, in the same gold thread, was trimmed with dark brown cord.

"You look just right," said Caroline approvingly. "And there's no need to rush. John's just heard we've got an extra quarter of an hour before Sir Henry arrives."

"Thank heaven for that!"

But if Sir Henry was unable to be there on time, the rest of Marlingham was extremely punctual. Small children, hungry, as John had predicted, from school, had to be shepherded away from trestle-tables laden with rolls, sandwiches, pies, tarts and cakes; everything, in fact, that could be made at the bakery, and for which orders could be placed with Mike, self-appointed order clerk for the occasion.

"The animals around here must be a very healthy lot!" observed Holly to Caroline, as they watched Mike settle himself at a table in the bakery on which had been placed a large notice saying 'Orders Taken'.

Caroline laughed. "He's in partnership with his father, who's very lenient about time off when Mike's seeing Abbie. They'd like them to settle down together as much as I would."

"I'm sure they will, eventually. They get on so well."

"They've known each other since they were children, but on Abbie's side it's been a case of familiarity not breeding contempt exactly, but certainly a taking for-granted attitude. Rather like John and Livvie Harding, I suppose. There is Livvie, by the way."

Immaculate in green and purple tweeds that immediately made Holly feel definitely over-dressed, Olivia had just parked a rakish scarlet sports car down the lane and was being helped out by John.

"Although I must say," Caroline continued, gazing at them thoughtfully, "that their feelings for each other seem to have changed just lately. They're certainly seeing each other a lot more often. She's a nice enough girl, but I've never been quite happy about her for John. But then, I'm probably biased! And this certainly isn't the moment to stand gossiping! I must go and make sure Abbie's ready for her spectacular first run. For some reason she's suddenly decided it would be nice to dress up for it in Victorian clothes. I told her it was only a bread-round and not the London to Brighton road-race, but you know Abbie!"

She went off, and Holly moved away

to persuade a group of children to stand somewhere else, other than by the food-tables. Not that she could blame them for clustering there like locusts; Abbie's pies looked particularly delicious.

A discreet cheering from the crowd now thronging Bun Lane announced the simultaneous arrival of a television van and the ice-cream van bearing Sir Henry. Clearly delighted at such an unexpected scoop, the television crew wasted no time in focusing their cameras as Sir Henry was handed down ceremoniously by John. He wore a tweed suit with a yellow, polo pullover, and was carrying an enormous ice-cream cornet which he immediately handed to the nearest small boy. Holly moved forward.

"Morning, my dear! Sorry to be late. Persuaded the driver to bring me straight here." He pressed a note into the ice-cream man's hand and personally made sure that he was able to reverse down the length of Bun Lane. "Obliging chap, but we don't want him selling ice-cream to this lot, do we? Ah, 'morning, Olivia,

my dear! All set when you are, Lorimer.
The sooner I can sink my teeth into one
of those delicious pies, the better!"

To renewed cheering and hand-
clapping, he mounted a rostrum made
up of a packing-case covered in red velvet
placed behind one of the reading-desks
from the Book Shop, and John swung
the old muffin-bell which Albert had
unearthed from a cupboard in the bakery.
A press photographer raised his camera,
and Albert and Buckie, immaculate in
snow-white overalls and bakers' caps,
stepped out into the lane.

'Our local celebrity' was how John
introduced Sir Henry, and the burst
of spontaneous applause that came from
the crowd seemed to surprise him. He
stood on the rostrum and looked around
him with what Abbie later described as
'a benevolent glare' and said,

"Very nice to be here! Afraid I may
have neglected you in the past. All going
to be different now that I shall be coming
to Marlingham to buy my bread!"

Holly had a sudden, vivid picture of

Sir Henry, basket over arm, doing the weekend shopping, then caught John's eye and glanced hastily away before she disgraced herself by giggling.

"We owe it all," Sir Henry continued, "to this little band of dedicated men and women who had the good sense and foresight to hold on to an important part of our country heritage — Marlingham Bakery!" There was more clapping. "Have great pleasure," Sir Henry concluded, "in declaring this bakery well and truly open. Though judging by what I can see on the tables, it's been open for quite a while already!" Clearly not a man to waste time on trivialities, he turned to John. "All right if we start eating now?"

John helped Sir Henry down from the rostrum, and then sprang up himself to say, "Help yourself everyone. Everything — rolls, buns, sandwiches, cakes and pies — have been made on the premises. Should you like what you eat, Mr. Michael Hawkins is in the bakehouse, ready to take your orders. The first delivery, by the way, will be made by

Miss Abigail Forbes in approximately ten minutes' time. Only a demonstration run today, but tomorrow she'll be out on her rounds from nine-thirty onwards willing to deliver anywhere in the town. And if you happen to live outside Marlingham, Mr. Buckie Willis will be happy to serve you." Out of the corner of his eye, he saw Sir Henry take an enormous bite out of a pie. "Enjoy yourselves!" he added quickly, but the words were lost in the rush to the tables.

"There's food in the cottage as well," he told Sir Henry, and led the way up the path and into the living-room, where Holly was already pouring coffee and passing plates.

"Nice little place you have here!" said Sir Henry, glancing around him appreciatively.

"It's only partly furnished as yet," said Holly.

"Come and have a browse through the Manor attics any time," Sir Henry offered. "Might be one or two things you could use. Only get woodworm if it's left."

"You've never suggested *I* should browse through your attics," said Olivia, arriving with Dr. Bellamy.

"You know you're welcome at any time, my dear," said Sir Henry.

Further conversation was prevented by the prolonged blowing of a hunting-horn out in the lane.

"Here comes Abbie!" said John. "This should be worth seeing."

They all hurried out into the garden again in time to see Abbie, wearing a long, crimson wool skirt under a closely fitting black velvet jacket, climb up on to the box of an old-fashioned tradesman's van. On her head was an enormous hat, whose curling brim held a veritable bouquet of pink velvet, cabbage-roses. On the side of the van, 'Baxters for Bread' was picked out in thick, gold lettering across the chocolate brown sides. Held at her head by Buckie, Daisy Belle was giving a creditable imitation of a veteran circus horse, an effect considerably enhanced by the ribbons and rosettes with which her harness had been decorated.

The television crew, half-eaten pies clamped between their jaws, zoomed in. Sir Henry, carried away by the excitement of the moment, cried, "Tally-ho! Gone away!" and was immediately button-holed by a red-haired young man with a microphone, who enquired if he would care to say a few words for the local radio station.

"Already said 'em!" Sir Henry pointed out.

"Will you really be eating nothing but Baxters' Bread from now on?" pursued the young man, undaunted.

"If" said Sir Henry, pointing at the trestles, bare now, except for some sad little sprigs of parsley, "they keep up this superb standard, I'd be a fool not to! So would you!"

"That should be worth a few extra orders!" John hissed into Holly's ear.

Blue jeans peeping out beneath her skirt, a garlanded whip in her hand,

Abbie was now up on the box.

"Where's Mike?" Caroline called urgently.

"Come on!" said John to Holly. "We'll take over from him. Let's hope he's been busy. Keep an eye on Sir Henry for us, Livvie!"

Mike was found, practically obscured by a queue of people waiting to place their orders, but he needed no urging to join Abbie. Through the open door Holly watched him mount the box and raise his cap to the cheering crowd; Daisy Belle prancing like a war-horse, meanwhile. All that's missing, thought Holly, is the confetti and the old shoe!

There came another tan-tivvy upon the horn, and the van lurched forward with Mike, to Caroline's obvious relief, holding the reins and Abbie waving demurely to the crowd.

Holly turned back to the table to help John. Fifteen minutes later they had dealt with the last order and were trying to assess the overall situation.

"I think we're home and dry," said

John. "As I thought, we can be sure of local support. But the orders from the villages will make all the difference. I've had some in already, and after today there should be more. Enough to keep Buckie fully occupied with the van."

"That's marvellous!" Holly stretched her arms above her head and flexed her aching fingers.

"It means there won't be any let-up for any of us," John warned. "Especially until the Baxters come back. And that won't be for a fortnight at the earliest."

"We'll make it," Holly assured him confidently.

"Still managing your London job by remote control?"

"There's not much to do at the moment. Far more interesting down here!"

"Am I speaking to the same young woman who, only a few weeks ago, actually claimed she couldn't even cope with a packet of bread-mix?"

"Well, no, not quite the same," Holly said.

"In what way different?" John glanced

up from numbering the orders in the ledger.

"It's not easy to say." Certainly, it wasn't only that she was now developing a taste for country life, for country pursuits and country people. It went much deeper than that. Suddenly, sitting there in the warm bakery, with Albert already assembling the ingredients for tomorrow's baking, Holly admitted to herself where the biggest difference lay. No longer was she in love with Brian but, in a way she had never experienced before, she loved this man now sitting beside her, with his quick but gentle humour, his ability to make even the most humdrum event seem exciting and his quiet consideration for other people. She smiled at him and he leaned towards her.

"Holly, my dear . . ."

"Darling!" came Olivia Harding's rich contralto behind them. "Henry's car has just arrived and he thinks he should be getting back. And I should be going, too."

Probably Olivia was the sort of person to whom endearments came easily, but the intimacy conjured up by that casual 'darling' seemed to be enough to take John's mind off what he had been about to say, and to bring him quickly to his feet. "Just coming, Livvie!" It was something, at least, that he remembered to hold out his hand to Holly and take her with him.

Sir Henry's limousine, with his chauffeur standing beside the open door, practically filled Bun Lane.

"Better be on my way. Enjoyed it enormously. Been chatting to a number of people. Think I may even open the grounds next year. Throw one or two garden thingummies. You'll have to help me arrange them, my dear." He patted Holly on the arm, "And don't forget to have a browse round my attics. Bring that young man of yours. Still haven't met him!"

"I will," Holly promised, thinking more of the attics than of Brian.

The car, with Livvie's on its tail, rolled

away down the lane between the little groups of people waiting presumably for Abbie's return. Holly glanced at her watch. They should have been back by now.

"I hope," said Caroline, coming up to her in some agitation, "that Daisy Belle hasn't bolted. I was afraid Abbie was giving her too many oats."

"I'm sure Mike would be able to handle her," said John. But unobtrusively he too glanced at his watch. "Just to be on the safe side I'll take the car and have a look for them, and Buckie can drive the van in the other direction." On his way to the car Holly saw him stop and speak to a couple of boys circling the lane on their bikes, obviously killing time until school started again. So, he was worried, too! Caroline looked as if she was on the verge of tears.

"Come on!" said Holly quickly. "You and I will start on the washing-up."

Even so, both of them, tea-cloths in hand, shot out into the lane when they heard John's car coming back. One look at his face told them the expedition had been fruitless. The next moment Buckie had turned into the lane. But he, too, shook his head when he saw them waiting.

"The police!" said Caroline. "I'm going to ring them!"

"Just a minute!" John put a restraining hand on her arm while he stared down the lane to where the two cyclists had now appeared. "I rather think a sighting's been made."

He was right. "We've found them!" called one cyclist.

"Where?" asked Caroline tautly, at the same moment that John said, "Are they all right?"

Obviously delighted to have such an attentive audience, the other cyclist took up the tale; not that he reached the point any faster than his friend.

"They were in a lane."

"In the ditch?"

"No, ma'am. Under some trees. The horse was eating the grass."

"Was it still between the shafts?"

Caroline was trembling with anxiety.

But for some reason the question had reduced the two to a state of almost hysterical laughter.

"Stop that!" snapped John.

The giggles ceased immediately. "The horse was still between the shafts, sir, and Miss Abbie and Mr. Hawkins were still in the van."

A slow smile began to dawn on Caroline's face. "Go on!" she invited.

"Well, they were sort of . . . of . . . "

"Kissing! Mr. Hawkins had his arms around Miss Abbie. And Miss Abbie was . . . "

"Yes, I see!" John interrupted quickly. "Thank you. You've been most helpful." He produced a couple of coins from his pocket, added, for good measure, two of Abbie's pies that had been hidden behind a coffee-urn, and sent them on their way.

"I think," said John to Caroline, "that we should call off the search-party, don't you?"

Her face was wreathed in smiles. "I do, indeed!"

Half an hour later an obviously well-fed Daisy Belle plodded placidly down Bun Lane, the reins loose upon her back, and stopped of her own accord outside the bakehouse. Up on the box Abbie and Mike sat very close. Abbie smiled mistily at her mother.

"Sorry to be so long," said Mike. "But I thought I should take advantage of Abbie's unusual, Victorian submissiveness to ask her to marry me."

"And she said yes?" breathed Caroline. "Oh, darling, I'm so pleased!"

"Oddly enough, so am I!" said Abbie, gazing fondly at Mike.

"This," said her uncle, "calls for a celebration. Leave the washing-up, Holly. Come on, Albert, Buckie — the oven can look after itself for half an hour. We're repairing to the Royal Oak!"

12

NEXT morning Holly set two alarm-clocks; one at five, the other at a quarter past. Still feeling guilty because she had overslept on the previous morning, she was determined to be up to make Albert a cup of tea when he came to light the oven fire. For it had been agreed that Albert should do the early turn for the first week at least.

"If it's all the same to you, Mr. Lorimer," he'd told John. "I'd be happier knowing everything was all right. And I've been getting up early every morning of my life. It's no hardship."

The same could hardly be said for Holly. Her immediate inclination when the first clock — borrowed from Caroline — shrilled out its message was to hurl it across the room, then roll over and sink back into oblivion.

But then she heard Albert coming up the lane.

With a mighty effort she sat up in bed, switched on her bedside lamp and reached for her clothes. At least, the cottage was still warm, even though the fire had not yet been started. She pulled on trousers and a thick pullover over her pyjamas and went sleepily down the stairs to put on the kettle.

While it was coming to the boil she unlocked and opened the front door; then shut it again quickly as a blast of cold air came in like a knife. But the brief glimpse she'd caught of her neglected garden in the light streaming from the windows of the bakery and the cottage made her slip on a warm jacket and open it again.

It was as if some invisible hand had wielded a gigantic, crystal spray. Not only was every twig, every withered cabbage-stalk, every blade of grass rimed in hoar-frost, but a thousand cobwebs were stretched like silver wire between the stems. It was an unexpected bonus for her early rising, and even the breath freezing in her nostrils didn't send her back indoors until the whistle of the kettle told her it was time to make the tea. And surely, on a morning like this, Albert would be glad of a hot drink.

She made it in a large thermos flask, picked up a bottle of milk from the stone floor of the tiny larder, and started for the bakery, picking her way carefully across the frosty cobbles. Why hadn't some previous owner thought to knock a door from the cottage into the bakery? Perhaps she'd put the question to Albert while he was drinking his tea.

He was astonished, but delighted, to see both her and the thermos flask. Pouring tea into his enormous mug and then watching while he cupped his hands before raising it to his lips was sufficient reward.

"Miss Holly, you shouldn't have done it, but I must say I enjoy a cup of tea first thing."

"What can I do to help, Mr. Higgins?" she asked, filling a mug for herself.

"Well, the fire's going well, though it'll be more than an hour before the oven's hot enough for Buckie to scuffle. I'll put the flour and yeast into the mixer and then we can sit and drink our tea while it's working."

They sat at one end of the table where the tins were stacked ready for the dough, and Holly asked Albert why there wasn't a connecting-door to the cottage.

He grinned. "There was one, once, miss. But the wife of the baker before the last had it bricked up. You can see the new bricks if you look in that far corner."

"But why?"

"Very houseproud she was. Reckoned it made too much mess, tramping straight in with flour on your boots."

"Goodness!" said Holly, impressed by such fastidiousness.

"Now that," said Albert thoughtfully, "would have been your Great-aunt Gertrude's sister-in-law, Maggie Pringle. She hadn't any children. More's the pity or she mightn't have been so

191

fussy! So the bakery came back to your great-aunt when her husband died. But she was in New Zealand by then, so it was let to Mr. Moss."

"And when did you come to work here?" prompted Holly, fascinated by these reminiscences.

"I caught the tail end of Mrs. Pringle, in a manner of speaking. Always on at me about wiping my feet, I remember, but a kind-hearted soul for all that. Every day she'd give me a fresh loaf to take home to my mother, and that meant a lot in those days. Not that I didn't work for it," he added sternly.

"No machines in those days," observed Holly mischievously, guessing the remark would bring a heated reaction.

"No, by gum!" said Albert. "We mixed every bit of dough by hand and then let it rise through the night, ready for first baking. And if there was going to be more than one baking — and there usually was — you'd mix another lot round about midnight."

"So you must have slept here, too?"

Albert let out a great bellow of laughter. "I'll say I did! We mixed the dough in a great trough, laid a plank across the top and I was put on it to sleep! Being no more than a lad, the force of the yeast would push up the plank and me with it! When I fell off we knew it was time to put the bread in! Didn't need these new-fangled alarm-clocks in those days, I can tell you!"

Holly laughed — as much with pleasure at the sight of the contentment on the old man's face as at the story itself.

"I must try it some time!" she said.

Suddenly the door was flung open, and John and Buckie came in on a great wave of cold air.

"Albert, you dark horse!" said John. "There was I thinking it was the call of duty that was getting you here so early, and all the time it was the thought of Miss Holly's company!"

"And the good cup of tea she makes!" said Albert gallantly. "Not that there's any call for her to wait on me. And there's no need for you to be so early either,

Mr. Lorimer! I've said I can manage, with Buckie to do the scuffling, and I mean it."

"I'm quite sure that you can," John told him. "But while we're such a small team, the more people that can do each other's jobs the better. After all, how could we have managed if we hadn't had you when the Baxters went into hospital?"

"Put like that," said Albert in a mollified tone, "it does make good sense. I can tell you one thing, though. If you're going to scuffle you'll need plenty of tea afterwards. There's nothing like it for giving a man a thirst."

"I can take a hint!" Holly got to her feet.

But this time she made it on the ring at the back of the bakery. And while she did she watched them punch the risen dough and cut it into lengths for the tins. Then Albert gravely inspected the bricks at the back of the oven and declared them to be sufficiently white-hot. Buckie dipped the scuffling-pole, with its piece of clean sacking tried on the end, into a pail of water and handed it to John who, with great care, began to wipe over the floor of the oven. From the violent sizzling as the water came into contact with the brick Holly could guess that the heat must be intense. Even she, standing back against the far wall, could feel the sweat pouring down her face.

While they slid the tins into the oven she poured the tea so that it was waiting for them once the door had been shut.

"Never," said John fervently after his first sip, "has a cup tasted so good!"

"Reckon you've earned it, too," said Albert approvingly. "You're quick to learn, Mr. Lorimer, and no mistake."

For answer, John collapsed on to a bench and mopped a handkerchief over his glistening forehead. "Do we have a breather now, Albert? Before we start on the next lot?"

Albert nodded. "About forty minutes before this batch is done and then the oven will have to be reheated. Miss Abbie coming down to make her pies later?"

"About eight o'clock, I think she said. And she'd appreciate Holly's help if that's possible."

Holly, to her extreme annoyance, suddenly let out an enormous yawn. Albert chuckled.

"I was expecting that, miss! Always happens the first few days before you get used to early rising. And the warmth of the oven doesn't help. What you need now is a couple of hours back in bed and then you'll be right as ninepence."

"But I can't possibly go back to bed now!" Holly protested.

"Oh yes you can!" said John firmly. "And I shall personally see that you do!"

He kept his word. At least, as far as her bedroom door, where he gave her a little push and said, "I'll give you two minutes while I fill a hot-water bottle, and then I'm coming to check that you're back between the sheets. And woe betide you if you're not!"

But she didn't need two minutes to strip off her sweater and slacks and crawl

196

back into the welcoming cocoon of her sleeping-bag. When John put his head round the door she was already asleep.

Without need of an alarm she awoke at a quarter to eight, greatly refreshed, and was washed and dressed and making toast in the kitchen when John put his head round the door.

"Good girl! How are you feeling?"

"Brilliant! But what sort of a baker's mate am I going to be if I can't get up early? I'm not a figure-head any longer you know."

"There's early — and *early!* And your body hasn't adjusted itself yet to your change of life-style. I don't suppose you went to sleep particularly early last night, either?"

She had to admit that she'd lain awake reviewing the events of the day until well after midnight.

While they'd talked John had cut himself a couple of slices of bread and put them under the grill. Bright sunshine pouring between Caroline's gay, gingham

197

curtains fell across the table on which she'd arranged her new crockery, and suddenly Holly was overwhelmed by the delightful domesticity of the situation. If only every day could begin like this!

And then, like a sort of tornado of happiness, Abbie was with them.

"Why didn't you tell me," she scolded Holly, "what a wonderful feeling it is to be engaged? Everyone being nice to you and wishing you well! You," she told her uncle, "must hurry up and join the club. Mustn't he, Holly?"

Holly managed a nod and a brief smile. But John himself, said, "Well, you never know. I might surprise you all one day."

Which, thought Holly despairingly, could mean only one thing.

That evening, just as dusk was falling, she sat in the kitchen leafing through a magazine Caroline had lent her and trying to work up sufficient strength to go and sweep out the bakery. Absorbed in an article about the conversion of an oast-house into a private dwelling, she was hardly aware of the darkness outside until a sudden, bloodcurdling scream made her jump up in alarm. Impossible to imagine anyone being attacked out there in the shadows of Bun Lane, but that was certainly what it had sounded like.

It came again when Holly was half-way to the door. Tearing it open she was just in time to see Albert slink across the yard and turn the corner of the bakehouse, a large, squealing bundle under one arm.

There was only one place he could be going to, down that path, and Holly began to shake with silent laughter as she realised that he must be carrying a baby pig en route to its new home in the bakery sty. But John and Mr. Baxter, she remembered, hadn't been over-enthusiastic about the idea. It would be interesting to see for how long Albert would be able to keep his secret to himself.

13

THE brown and gold of 'Baxters for Bread' became a familiar sight in Marlingham during the days that followed, with Abbie making new friends wherever she went. The aura of happiness surrounding Mike and herself seemed to influence everybody and everything. Beautifully baked bread — even that mixed by John! — came out of the oven, and Abbie's pastry was feather light. Holly, trained as her assistant, became so proficient she actually took over the preparation of the pies while Abbie was out on her rounds. The van ran sweetly from the second the ignition-key was turned, and Daisy Belle was good as gold.

There came a period of exceptionally mild weather, and Holly was delighted to see the green spears of unidentified bulbs pushing through the soil beneath the living-room window. It seemed incredible that Christmas was only weeks away and that Abbie was already taking orders for Christmas cakes.

Holly felt happy and fulfilled. Like John, she was learning something new, and enjoying every moment of it. She had now grown used to rising early each morning, and the days were hardly long enough to contain the variety of duties she had to perform. Every evening found her exhausted but happy — and she wasn't alone in this. Caroline, John, Abbie and Mike were all, somehow, managing to do two jobs at once; and Albert and Buckie were being called upon to work far harder than either had expected when they'd first said they would like to come back to the bakery. But it was all gloriously worth while, for orders were continuing to pour in.

Apart from the preparation of hurried meals eaten, more often than not standing up, Holly spent little time in Rosemary Cottage, but, even so, she was able to make small additions to its comfort.

There was the set of patchwork cushions, for instance, that she found at a sale of work in Marlingham's church hall when she was delivering some cakes for the produce stall, and which she carefully washed and pressed. And the old tapestry fire-screen from the same source.

Old Albert obligingly found a couple of wheel-backed chairs in his workshop and spent his spare time while the bread was baking in whittling new staves where the old ones had rotted. Sand-papered down, painted with a clear varnish and given the patchwork cushion-covers, they made a perfect pair of dining-room chairs.

"I'll look out for a couple more," Albert promised. "And a good, solid table to go with them."

Not to be beaten, Buckie arrived one morning proudly bearing an enormous rag rug that his grandmother had made to counteract the shortages of the Second World War. "She was throwing it out," he explained, "but I told her it was just the sort of thing Miss Holly would like for her old cottage."

"You're so right," said Holly gratefully. "Please thank her very much indeed. And thank you for bringing it." And she laid it lovingly down upon the floor of the little hall, where its colours, muted by the years, blended with the old red tiles which one day, she promised herself, she would get down on her hands and knees and polish.

Even Mike Hawkins' mother sent a pair of brass candlesticks as a house-warming present, and Sir Henry, a couple of days after the opening, sent over a large, brown-paper parcel, containing a pair of long, brown velvet curtains.

'Thought these might be useful,' said the note that came with them. 'Old buildings are beautiful but notoriously draughty!'

Holly hung them in her living-room over the doors leading to the hall and kitchen, and felt the benefit immediately.

And the appearance of the outside of the cottage was improving, too. Whenever Buckie had a few minutes to spare he would seize a spade and 'dig Miss Holly's patch'. Sometimes it was only a couple of feet, but often it was more, and Holly began to think of seed catalogues and fertilisers.

Soon, she promised herself, she would throw a house-warming party for all her kind friends and benefactors, but at the moment there was no time for anything but unremitting hard labour.

She saw little of Brian, her hasty trips to town nearly always coinciding with his journeys abroad. Brief reports from Jill in New York told of exciting new contacts and the possibility of her staying out there permanently; on the understanding, of course, that Holly would join her. Only a few weeks ago she would have been wildly excited at the suggestion, but now the prospect left her singularly unmoved. Her present horizons were limited to Rosemary Cottage and the Old Bakery — and, of course, her fellow-workers.

Inevitably she saw a great deal of John, but nearly always in the company of one or more of the others. They were now back on their old familiar footing, and only now and again would he seem quiet and withdrawn; these occasions, Holly had noticed, nearly always occurred after one of Olivia Harding's frequent visits to the Book Shop or the Bakery. It was as if he were trying to make up his mind upon some important matter. And it wasn't difficult to guess what that was. The wonder of it was that he hadn't decided, years ago, to ask her to marry him.

One morning Holly woke before the alarm, and lay for a moment listening to the familiar sounds from the yard; the clanking of buckets at the pump, the scrape of wheels on stone as Buckie manhandled the cart out of the barn, John's cheery whistle as he came up the lane. But this morning the sounds were muted by the scudding of heavy raindrops against the window-pane. The fine weather had broken at last.

And with it seemed to slip away the good fortune they had enjoyed. Things — some trivial, some important — began to go wrong, although even the important ones seemed, at the time, to be more funny than tragic.

It began with the escape of Albert's pig. Afterwards, it was discovered that everyone, even John, knew of the animal's existence, but that no-one had mentioned it in case objections were raised. And it was — at least, until that cold winter's day when it escaped — a very nice little pig! So when the cry was first raised by Buckie — "Pig's out!" — no-one stopped to ask 'What pig?' but immediately dropped whatever they were doing and set off in pursuit.

"He's in the square," said Buckie. "I spotted him as I drove through."

Albert, who had been filling a bucket at the pump, had a head start on everyone else, so it was impossible to see if his expression held guilt as well as concern. Next came Holly, Abbie and Buckie in a tight, chattering group, and last of all, having had the forethought to find a sack, came John.

Fortunately, Pig was still in the square,

apparently absorbed in pre-Christmas window-shopping. Hypnotised by his reflection in the window of 'Miss Moggs, High Class Milliner', he seemed quite unaware that they were creeping up behind him, until Albert pounced. But not quickly enough. With a frenzied wriggle he was off across the square like a bright pink rocket, squealing at the top of his voice. Shoppers side-stepped nimbly, and shopkeepers came out of their doorways.

"Don't just stand there! Come and help!" called Abbie.

Several people obeyed her command and, when Pig took refuge at the bottom of the grocer's area steps, they barred the exit as Albert and John went down with the sack.

But even with the odds so heavily weighted against him, Pig didn't give in easily. It took at least five minutes of lunging with the open sack from one end of the area to the other, to the accompaniment of guidance and encouragement shouted from those hanging over the railings, before he was finally caught. To a round of applause Albert carried him in the sack back up the steps.

"Thank you all for your help," said John. "I sincerely hope the excitement's over for the afternoon."

On the way back up Bun Lane he remarked casually to Albert, "You know, what this pig needs is company. That's probably why he ran away and why he was staring so hard into the shop window. He thought he'd found a mate! I'm sure the sty's big enough for two."

Albert looked at him gratefully. "Thanks, Mr. Lorimer!"

The smell of burning had reached Holly's nostrils as they'd turned into the lane, but it wasn't until they'd nearly reached the bakehouse that Albert suddenly stopped in his tracks, sniffed the air like an old war-horse, then clapped his hand to his forehead.

"My bread!" he groaned. "It should have come out fifteen minutes ago!" He started to run, but John laid a restraining hand upon his shoulder.

"You take this little chap back to his sty. Buckie and I will deal with the bread."

'Dealing with the bread' meant disposing of countless charred fragments, but by the time a shamefaced Albert had returned the fire had already been relit and Buckie was up in the loft pouring more flour down the chute.

"We'll soon catch up," John assured Albert. "Don't worry!"

The extra afternoon baking had been laid on to meet the requirements of a nearby boarding-school for packed lunches on the following day, but fortunately there was still time to meet the deadline. Although it did mean, of course, the complete write-off of one whole baking.

"However," John observed that evening after Albert and Buckie had gone home and he, Holly and Abbie were chuckling over the event, "at least Pig's now out in the open, so to speak, and we can all go and talk to him when we've got a minute to spare. The poor little chap must have been very lonely out there on his own.

To redress the balance, the next catastrophe, two days later, was entirely John's fault. Insisting that everyone, in spite of the acute shortage of workers, must have an occasional day off, he was working Albert's early turn for him. After lighting the fire and putting the ingredients into the electric mixer, he switched on the machine and immediately went outside to take Pig his breakfast. And even at six o'clock on a frosty morning one couldn't leave Pig without at least a token session of back-scratching.

John's return to the bakehouse coincided with Holly's arrival, and the two of them stood in the doorway, transfixed by the sight of globules of some glistening white substance flying through the air and raining down on to the bakery floor. And not only the floor. Every surface was covered and, as they watched, the globules, like some terrifying science-fiction film, began to grow steadily larger.

John leaped across the floor and

turned off the switch of the mixing machine. "I couldn't have put the catch on properly!"

Investigation proved him right. As the big drum had revolved, the lid had come open and the contents had come — literally — flying out. And the yeast, of course, had continued to do its work, no matter where it was!

"I think," said Holly faintly, "that a sweeping brush is called for. Then out into the lane, don't you think?"

"Thank goodness Albert's got the day off," said John feelingly. "Or I would never live it down."

Fifteen minutes later the bakery was reasonably clean, but the yard looked as if it had just experienced an early fall of snow. Buckie, coming up the lane soon afterwards, was shouted at to wipe his boots.

"Or we'll have it all back in again," said Holly feelingly.

Afterwards, over coffee and toast in the kitchen of Rosemary Cottage, they had a hilarious time telling Abbie about

211

it, but all the same, another precious sack of flour had been wasted.

"Wonder how that got there!" said Albert next day as he scooped a gobbet of dough from a ledge that Holly had overlooked. She caught John's eye and he began to laugh.

"Well, Albert," he began, "it was like this . . ."

"Happened to me once!" Albert confessed when the story had ended.

"Well, thank goodness for that!" said John in a relieved tone.

They all laughed, and Holly was aware of a growing bond between the members of the bakery work-force that could reduce all their calamities to a humorous level. Or almost all.

The following day Daisy Belle had an attack of colic and had to be rested. To do both town and country deliveries, the van had to work overtime and the engine became more and more sluggish.

"Reckon it needs a new carburettor," said Buckie. "We'll have to get one from Aylesbury."

"Right!" said John. "I'll go in tomorrow morning after we've baked."

But next morning, due to a misunderstanding about shift-times between John and Buckie, the fire was never lit, and Albert, coming in to start the mixing, found only a cold oven. The repercussions couldn't have been much worse. It was nearly three hours later before the bread was ready.

In Marlingham itself this didn't matter very much, but John, ringing round the village shops to explain the delay, was told regretfully that the delivery would be too late because most of the villagers would already have bought their bread from the travelling shop. It was the first that John had heard of a travelling shop.

"Oh, yes," he was told, "it started a couple of days after you opened your bakery, and doing quite well we understand."

It was an expensive mistake. That afternoon John carefully typed out a daily rota of duties so that there could

213

be no repetition of the incident.

"It was something I'd intended doing," he told Holly when he called in at Rosemary Cottage in the evening, "but I just never got around to it. The danger now, of course, is that we're all getting tired and more apt to make mistakes and forget things. It only needs something like this to happen again and the villages will lose faith altogether and cancel their orders. And I can't say that I would blame them."

He was leaning forward in his chair, his hands stretched out to the cheerful blaze in the inglenook. Behind him, the firelight made moving shadows upon the pale walls, and the mimosa Holly had brought back from her last visit to London released a heady fragrance into the warm air.

"It's so restful here!" he said suddenly. "I don't know how we'd manage without you, Holly."

Admittedly, he'd said 'we' and not 'I' but, even so, she was so moved by his remark she felt treacherous tears prick her eyelids; she, too, was beginning to feel the strain of the pressure they were working under. Quickly she got to her feet. "I'll go and make us some coffee."

"Try not to worry," she said when she came back with a laden tray and now in complete control of her feelings. "I'm sure it won't happen again."

"I sincerely hope not! Otherwise we won't be able to start repaying our creditors by the agreed date. They were very short-term loans you know."

"Surely they're not agitating for the money?"

"Of course not. And I'm sure they never would. But a bargain's a bargain, for all that."

"You're tired," she said. "After a good night's sleep, everything will seem different."

He gave her a wry smile. "A good night's sleep is just what I'm *not* going to have. It's Albert's brother's birthday today and they'll probably make a night of it. So I'm lighting the fire in the morning."

"Do you," she asked quietly, "sometimes wish you'd never bumped into me in the square on that Saturday night? If you hadn't none of this would have happened."

He looked at her. "I'll never regret meeting you, Holly. And the Bakery was just the challenge I needed to get me out of my nice, comfortable rut."

"You can't have much time for writing, these days," she pointed out.

"That's true! But the rest is probably doing my creative faculties a power of good. By the way, I heard this morning my book has definitely been accepted for publication, and there's even talk of an American paperback edition."

"John, that's marvellous! I'm so pleased! Why didn't you tell me before?"

"I meant to, but then all this trouble started and everything else faded from my mind."

"I'm so pleased!" she said again.

"And I'm pleased that you're pleased!"

She was kneeling on the hearth-rug, having just thrown an armful of logs on to the dying flames, and now she turned to him, her cheeks flushed, her eyes glowing with excitement. Suddenly, he reached out an arm and pulled her towards him. Then took her face between his hands and kissed her, gently but thoroughly, full upon the mouth. Once again she felt ecstasy filling both her body and her mind, as if physical passion moved side by side with mental fulfilment. And this time *he* had kissed *her!* He took his lips away and slid his hands down on to her shoulders, and she felt that he was trembling. Or was it only the violent beating of her own heart that made it seem so?

"Holly, I'm sorry! I shouldn't have done that!"

She opened her mouth to say that, as far as she was concerned, there was no earthly reason why he should not have kissed her. And why, oh why, had he stopped?

And then the heavy iron knocker on the front door of the cottage was used by an impatient hand. They drew away from each other, and Holly, feeling exhilaration drain from her body, got slowly to her feet and went, with dragging steps, to open the door.

"Thought you were never coming!" said Abbie cheerfully. "Your beloved has just been on the phone up at the house. Wants you to ring him back at once. He rang the Bakery, but I imagine you don't hear it through these walls."

"No, I'm afraid I don't," said Holly, fighting for composure. "And it's locked up now."

"Well, stop looking so sad about it," said Abbie vigorously, "and come up to the shop and ring him. It sounded urgent."

"Holly," said Brian, his voice bubbling with elation over the telephone, "it's happened just as I planned. I've landed old Medlicott's job!"

"Congratulations!" She felt genuinely pleased for him, although nothing like the pleasure she'd experienced at hearing of John's book.

"Thanks, darling! Any chance of you coming up to celebrate?"

"'Fraid not! Things aren't going too well down here at the moment."

"What's happened?"

Briefly she explained about the misunderstanding of shift-times and the consequent abortive deliveries.

"Bad luck!" But clearly he wasn't deeply concerned. "By the way, I shall be handling the Jarvis account now, so I may be seeing Sir Henry after all."

"Won't you deal with the man who handles his advertising?"

"Normally, yes. But I thought I might mention your name and get a personal interview with the boss. You wouldn't mind would you?"

London and Brian's affairs seemed impossibly remote; all that mattered at the moment were Marlingham and the future of the bakery. "No, I don't mind," she said.

She replaced the receiver, then put her head round the sitting-room door.

"Brian's been promoted," she told Caroline, Abbie and John.

"Congratulations!" said John politely.

"That's lovely, dear," said Caroline warmly.

"Soon be able to keep you in the manner to which you've grown accustomed!" said Abbie.

Holly half-hoped that John would offer to walk her back to the cottage, but it was Abbie who got to her feet, saying, "Mind if I sleep at the cottage tonight, Holly? I want to make an early start on the pies tomorrow, and it's so much easier to roll out of bed and straight into the nice, warm bakery than feel my way down Bun Lane in the dark! You don't know how lucky you are! I've got my sleeping-bag and tooth-brush, so I won't be any trouble!"

"You'd never be that!" Holly assured her. "And I'd be glad of the company. Goodnight, Caroline! Goodnight, John!"

"Goodnight, dear!" said Caroline. "Sleep well!"

John got to his feet and saw them

off, but there was no indication in his manner towards Holly that he regretted the interruption of their conversation at the cottage. On the contrary, he was now in complete control of himself.

14

NEXT morning the van wouldn't start at all. No amount of coaxing and persuading could get more than a feeble whine out of her, and even that gave up in the end.

"And I never went into Aylesbury to collect a new carburettor," said John, furious with himself.

"You couldn't," Holly reminded him. "The oven wasn't heated on time and you were catching up on the baking with Albert."

"So I was!" They were standing in the yard beside the van, watching Buckie tinker under the bonnet. He drew out his head and looked at John.

"Sorry, boss! It's no good. It's got to have a new carburettor."

"Then you'd better drop everything, catch the next bus and go in and get one."

"But how will you manage the deliveries?"

"Daisy Belle!" said John. "Mike's passed her as fit for normal duties. If one sort of horse-power is going to let us down, the other can take over! Holly, if you come with me, we should be able to cut the town delivery time by half."

"Of course! But will Albert and Abbie be able to manage on their own?"

During the last couple of days she'd been helping more and more in the bakery.

"They'll have to!"

Holly frowned in concentration. "John, wouldn't it be more sensible to deliver to the village shops first before the factory bread gets there, and do the town this afternoon?"

He shook his head. "It's a good idea, Holly, but I don't think we will. You see, Marlingham depends upon us for all its bread. Mrs. Foster at the stores agreed to stop taking pre-packed bread when we opened the bakery. And whatever happens Baxters will go on baking bread for the townsfolk. I'm afraid it's a case of you and I dashing in and out of houses like a pair of robots. No time for chats this morning!"

At least the rain had stopped. The crisp, wintry sunshine seemed to generate a sort of feverish energy in both Holly and John, and Daisy Belle couldn't have been more co-operative. She stood docily when required, then obligingly moved on to the next house of her own accord, thus allowing them to practically sprint from door to door with their baskets. As John had said, there was no time for chat; a quick greeting, a hurried 'pay me tomorrow', and they were on their way. To their great satisfaction they arrived back at the bakery half an hour ahead of Abbie's usual schedule.

But there was still no time for more than a quick cup of coffee and a nosebag for Daisy, while the racks of fresh rolls and bread were slid into the van. In half an hour they were on their way again, bound for the first village.

Everything went smoothly until they

reached a place, about a mile outside the town, where the railway line crossed the road. As they approached it they heard the sound of the warning bell ringing down the line. Had they been in the van they could easily have accelerated and crossed before the barrier descended. But they were seated behind Daisy Belle's broad, shining rump as she clip-clopped along at an easy trot. The barrier came down practically upon her nose and she backed a couple of indignant paces.

"Steady, Daisy! Won't be long!"John assured her.

In fact it could only have been two minutes before the engine came into sight, but it seemed more like two hours. John breathed a sigh of relief. As the coaches slid past he gathered up the reins in readiness. But the train suddenly glided to a halt — with the last coach still on the crossing. "Now what's happening?"

What did happen was that the whole train immediately went into reverse and rumbled back the way it had come. But this time it was the leading coach that halted in front of Daisy Belle's quivering nostrils.

"At least," John said, "I can now ask the driver why he's behaving in such a crazy fashion."

Handing Holly the reins he jumped off the box and went to consult with the men in the driver's cabin. Two minutes later he was back.

"The next piece of line is single track, apparently, and there's a train coming the other way that has to pass first. And it's late! We could be here for *hours!*"

It wasn't a matter of hours, but by the time the other train had arrived and the barrier was eventually lifted many valuable minutes had been lost.

Whether it was because she was growing tired, or because standing still for so long had robbed her of her impetus, Daisy Belle now refused to trot but plodded on at a steady, but desperately slow, walk. And the gradient of the road began to rise steeply.

"I'll walk up the hill," said John, "that

226

might help her a bit." And he threw the reins on to the horse's back and jumped on to the road; not a difficult feat at the speed Daisy was travelling.

"We both will," said Holly, and followed him down.

Daisy gave them what could have been a grateful look, but she wasn't, even so, inspired to greater efforts.

It was impossible to tell if she was genuinely tired or just pulling their legs. Certainly, her own looked sound enough when they walked behind to check.

At the top of the hill they mounted the box once more, while Daisy snatched a quick, reviving mouthful from the hedgerow. It was a pity, Holly thought, that they had such urgent matters on their minds, for the view from this vantage-point was superb. The whole of Buckinghamshire seemed to stretch before them in a patchwork of fields and woodland, with the occasional gleam of a stream or lake and the blue line of the Chilterns always in the distance. Daisy Belle began the long descent to the cluster of red-tiled roofs which was their destination.

They had covered about half the distance when Holly suddenly pointed to a black and white-striped van speeding along a main road towards the village. "Isn't that the travelling shop?"

John shaded his eyes. "Oh, heavens! So it is! And now it will be ahead of us all the way." He drew Daisy Belle to a halt. "If it hadn't been for that train we would have made it."

"It is a shop," Holly pointed out. "Maybe there'll be enough customers to keep it waiting while we get on to the next place."

"Not a hope," said John. "It's on the only road through the village so it's sure to see us and put on a spurt. Anyway, I'm worried about Daisy. It really doesn't seem as if she's fit enough to stand the pace."

"Well," said Holly, determined not to let him become too dejected, "it was worth a try."

"I suppose so."

In silence he turned the cart and they began the journey home. But when they'd reached the top of the hill leading down to the level-crossing John stopped the cart and let Daisy crop the grass on the roadside. Then he reached behind him, selected a couple of buns from the tightly packed trays, and handed one to Holly. "We may as well cut our losses!"

They munched in silence for a while, and then Holly asked, "What do we do now? Try again tomorrow if Buckie's got the van working?"

He shook his head. "From what was said the other day I'm sure we're going to get back to telephone messages cancelling the orders. And if that is the case we shall just have to be less ambitious and concentrate on Marlingham, and hope that we manage to keep going for the next few weeks. But things will be critical for a time I'm afraid."

"I'm sure our backers would wait a little while longer," said Holly.

"I don't want to ask them to. I

229

happen to know that at least two of them are in urgent need of the money. Ralph Bartlett needs it to replace old farm machinery and Tim Johnson has a growing tribe of youngsters to feed and educate. And, nearer home, Mike and Abbie will soon be wanting to set up on their own."

"Sir Henry?" Holly suggested. "He was very interested in the bakery."

"Yes — there's always Sir Henry." John stared thoughtfully down the hill to where a train was now tearing non-stop across the crossing. "But I'd rather not, for personal reasons, ask Sir Henry at the moment."

"Yes, I see," said Holly, although she didn't, in fact, see at all. Could it be because Sir Henry might mention it to Olivia? And, in John's eyes at least, that could seem like an admission of defeat. Her good opinion of him would certainly be important to him.

"I'd much rather," John continued, "put Operation Longstop, as my solicitor called it, into action."

"What on earth's that?" asked a mystified Holly.

"Well, when we started this business provision obviously had to be made in case it turned out to be a dreadful flop and everyone lost their jobs and their money. And since it was all my idea I felt I should be the one to do it."

"Was that what Mr. Boucher meant when he told me that steps had been taken to cover the possible dissolution of the firm?"

"That sounds like a nice, polite way of describing bankruptcy, but that's the general idea. Well, most of my capital is invested in the shop and in Abbie's tea-room, but I do happen to own a small but very valuable collection of first editions. My great-great-grandfather began it, and it's been added to by subsequent generations ever since. They've now been valued and are worth a small fortune. More than sufficient to bear the running costs of the bakery for several months, if necessary, while we get on our feet again. *And* to repay our creditors in full."

And to think, thought Holly, that Brian had once doubted the motives of this man! Aloud, she said vehemently, "But you can't, you simply can't sell your inheritance like that! I'm sure your father wouldn't have approved."

"On the contrary, my father was a great romantic. He would consider them well lost for love of . . . a . . . " For some reason, he hesitated, and it was Holly who finished his sentence for him.

" . . . . for love of a country bakery? I find that hard to believe."

For a moment he said nothing, simply fixing her with a thoughtful gaze that seemed to be trying to tell her that she didn't know the whole story about his father. Had there, she wondered, been some great romantic love in his life? Had he been so utterly devoted to John's mother that . . .

"My father," said John suddenly, "would have approved of you. But he wouldn't have approved of the way I've treated you."

"Why?" For a second Holly raised panic-stricken eyes to his. Surely he hadn't realised the true extent of her feelings for him? But her anxiety was short-lived.

"Persuading you not to sell Rosemary Cottage and the bakery. Persuading you to come down and help us, and making you work like a slave ever since you got here."

"You're not to talk such nonsense! I'm here because I *want* to be here and for no other reason. I'm loving every minute at the bakery and, as for Rosemary Cottage, thank heavens you stopped me from selling it!"

"Well, that makes me feel a little better." He'd taken her hand in his, and now he turned it over and stared down at it. Almost absent-mindedly he bent his head and kissed the palm, then folded her fingers over it. Then he gave it back to her.

"We'd better be going. But thank you

for listening. I feel more capable now of facing the music and doing what has to be done."

During the journey home her fingers stayed curled over the place where his lips had touched her palm. Perhaps, after all, her love was reciprocated, just a little.

"Would you mind," John asked as they turned into the square at Marlingham, "taking Daisy and the van back to the bakery, while I pop into the shop to see if what I fear has happened? Tell Albert we'll try and get rid of some of the bread at the café. And if Mike's there, would you get him to have a look at Daisy? Otherwise, phone him. I'll be down later to find how Buckie's got on with the van and to tell you the worst."

After she had explained the situation to Albert, seen Mike and learned there was nothing the matter with Daisy Belle — "She's not normally asked to climb hills, so she was probably on her high horse! If you see what I mean!" — she checked with Buckie that the van was almost finished, and then went into the cottage. There, she found a cable from the States:

'Flying back Thursday. Have great offer of jobs for both. Get packing Jill.'

She stood with the cable in her hands, thinking how, just a few weeks ago, she would have been wild with excitement at the thought of going to America to work. Now, compared with the prospect of transforming the cottage into a place of homely beauty, and the bakery into a busy, self-supporting family business, the opportunity offered little satisfaction. Even so, she'd have to go up to London tomorrow and get everything ready for Jill's return; and the sooner she told John about her change of plans the better.

"I'll take a couple of baskets of this bread up to the café," she told Albert. "Perhaps Buckie could bring some, too, when he's finished."

This, she thought, as she hurried up the lane, could be the beginning of a proper confectioner's shop in Marlingham;

if only they could survive the next few weeks without John having to sell his precious books.

Caroline told her that John was in his study and confirmed that there had been several telephone calls for him. The study lay down a short corridor leading out of the book shop. Holly walked towards the open door, then stopped abruptly. John wasn't alone. But it was hardly surprising that she hadn't heard voices. Leaning back in his arms, Olivia Harding was smiling up at him.

"I had no idea," she was saying, in a voice vibrant with emotion, "that I could be so happy!"

For answer, John pulled her close so that he stood with her head nestling under his chin. And then she lifted it so that her face, like the upturned flower of some exotic plant, was very near to his.

"Dear John, you've been very patient with me, letting me ramble on while I sorted out exactly what I wanted."

In a moment, Holly knew, his lips

would come down upon her mouth, just as, once, they had covered hers. She could bear no more. As silently as she had come she turned and fled.

No wonder he'd sometimes seemed so remote and withdrawn. Waiting on tenter-hooks for Olivia's answer, the additional worry of the bakery must have been an almost insupportable burden. Well, if there was disappointment on that score, there would be happiness on this. She wondered how long it would be before they made their engagement public. This evening, perhaps, when they held the little staff meeting that was beginning to be a weekly occurrence.

15

THAT evening Holly was deliberately late for the meeting at John's house. At least she could spare herself the anguish of hearing him announce his engagement to Olivia. But, to her surprise, she found that he'd waited for her arrival before beginning the meeting and that there was none of the air of celebration that she'd expected. John, in fact, looked at his most grim.

"I wanted to put you all in the picture," he began as Holly, with a murmured apology for her lateness, slid into a chair. "You all know what happened this morning. As a result the village shops have cancelled their orders and, up until an hour ago, things didn't look too good for the firm. However, the situation has been unexpectedly retrieved from disaster by the intervention of one person."

He paused, and Holly thought — Olivia

has decided to invest in the company. What could be more reasonable? Naturally she would wish to share in her husband's interests. It would be treachery on her part to feel anything but profound relief at the news. But it was with difficulty that she gave John what she hoped was an encouraging smile.

"We owe it all," he continued, his face expressionless, "to Holly. And to her fiancé, Brian Redfearn."

There came murmurs of surprise from the others, and Holly felt her smile sag. "He, knowing more about these things than any of us," John continued, "has just telephoned me and explained that he visited Sir Henry Jarvis this afternoon, after being given permission by Holly, and persuaded him into an agreement whereby the bakery will supply one of his London canteens with regular deliveries of bread, buns and anything else that we can provide. What is more, transport will be provided, so that we shall have no worries on that score. Not to put too fine a point upon it, the situation has been saved at the eleventh hour by Holly realising, better than I, where our salvation lay."

For a moment he gave way to the babble of delighted voices, and then added, "I think that's all I can tell you for the moment. I gather that one of Sir Henry's executives will ring me in the morning to arrange details, but the arrangements won't come into operation until next week, when, I understand, Mr. and Mrs. Baxter should be back with us."

As the meeting broke up everyone converged upon Holly with excited congratulations. "That lad of yours isn't just a pretty face," said Abbie approvingly, "he's got brains as well."

Holly parried their remarks as best she could, then looked around for John. The sooner she explained that she'd known nothing of Brian's actions the happier she would be. Obviously he thought that the initiative had come from her; an unforgivable course of action for her to take without prior consultation with himself. No wonder he'd looked so grim! She must clear up the misunderstanding at once. But he must have slipped away when the others had been engaging her attention. She went out into the hall.

John was at the front door, opening it to usher in a windblown but laughing Olivia.

"Thought you were never coming to let me in!"

"Sorry, Livvie! We were having a meeting." With his arm around her, he drew her inside and bent to kiss her cheek. "Come into the study and I'll organise some coffee. You're frozen!"

Holly turned and went quickly into the kitchen. What did it really matter now what John thought of her? She wouldn't be staying.

Caroline was already filling the percolator. "Caroline, I won't wait for coffee. I've got to be back in London tomorrow, so I've things to do. Tell John for me, would you, in case I don't manage to see him before I go? I'll be in touch."

Walking back down Bun Lane she decided to ring Brian from the bakery.

"Holly, my sweet! I thought you'd ring!" He sounded enormously pleased with himself.

"Did you?"

"You don't sound very cheerful."

"Oh, I'm fine! Just a little puzzled. John only gave us the bare outline of your discussions with Sir Henry. I wondered if you could fill in the details."

"Pleasure! I saw him this afternoon. Mentioned your name, and it worked like a charm. The old boy's really taken a shine to you."

"I like him, too," said Holly stoutly. "What happened then?"

"Well, I happened to mention you were having trouble at the bakery, and he was very concerned. At first he just reached for his cheque-book, but I said it wasn't so much a question of money as of finding an easier outlet for your products. Right?"

"Right!" said Holly.

Brian had, indeed, put his finger

accurately upon the heart of the problem.

"And then I told him that he had the perfect solution in his own hands. You see, I happened to know from a friend of mine that one of his companies had just taken over a new office block in the suburbs — not all that far from Marlingham — and were about to send out tenders for the canteen catering. So why didn't he ask you to provide delicious crusty bread and home-made, country pies and whatever else you could produce? And he jumped at the idea."

"That was very clever of you, Brian."

"Yes, wasn't it! It's all been laid on from Wednesday week. Just needs your agreement."

"John's, really."

"You are pleased, aren't you?"

"Of course!"

"Thought you would be! When are you coming up?"

"Tomorrow, actually." And she told him about Jill's cable although not, at this point, about the offer of work in the

243

States. That would have to be broken to him later.

"Good!" he said. "We can celebrate my promotion and the bakery's survival."

When she'd put down the receiver she locked up the bakery and went back into the cottage. The cablegram lay where she'd left it on the kitchen table, and she read it through again. Accepting the job in the States now seemed the sensible thing to do. The only thing in fact.

To her surprise Brian, too, approved. "The agency has a subsidiary in New York," he told her on the following evening, when they were dining at his favourite restaurant. "If I play my cards properly I should be able to get over there fairly often."

"You may not want to see me after hearing what I have to tell you," she said wearily. Ever since leaving Marlingham that morning she'd been moving in a kind of trance, automatically doing the routine office jobs before Jill came back, and afterwards going back to her flat to change for her date with Brian; but one thing she'd been quite definite about in her mind. Brian must be made to realise, once and for all, that marriage was out of the question. Impossible to marry him, now, knowing that she loved John even if there was no possible chance of her love ever being returned.

"What do you have to tell me?" he asked.

"Brian, I'm terribly sorry but I can't possibly marry you now."

To her astonishment he nodded understandingly. "I thought that's how you would feel! New job, new country, new life-style. The last thing you'll want is to be tied to someone in England."

She could only stare at him in astonishment at this easy acceptance of something that had worried her all day. But at least his complete misunderstanding of her reason for breaking their brief engagement was sparing her the emotional scene she had dreaded.

"I'd be the same myself" he assured her. "But I shall still want you to be free to see me when I'm over there, of course. If I were you I should insist on having your own apartment — don't share with Jill. And then, when I'm in New York, I can stay with you. No need to worry about the neighbours then!"

His meaning was abundantly clear, and it took all her strength of will not to betray the distaste she felt.

"How about Christmas?" he asked. "Will you still be able to manage Switzerland?"

"I don't know yet how soon Jill wants me in New York," she said, fingers crossed beneath the tablecloth.

But her fears on that score were dispelled next day when a sleeker, smoother and altogether more sophisticated Jill told her all about it. It was, in every sense, to be an exchange.

"The New York fashion editor and her assistant are to fill our posts, and you and I, Holly, will be filling theirs! It's all so beautifully simple. I've already had the American end explained to me, and told

Louella what to expect over here, and you'll do the same with your opposite number when she arrives."

"And when do we actually go?" Holly asked.

"Well, I go tomorrow week, and you join me whenever you're ready. The beauty of it is we can even swop cars and apartments if you're agreeable. Much more convenient for everyone."

"Much!" Holly echoed, her mind working furiously. It was certainly a sensible arrangement. And in many ways it would be better to go quickly, like this. There would be no time to go back to Marlingham; a quick telephone call answered by Caroline, if she was lucky to ask if they would keep an eye on the cottage for her until she returned, with no mention of when that might be. And it really wouldn't matter now, she thought tiredly, if John never knew that Brian had acted entirely upon his own initiative when he'd approached Sir Henry.

"You'll love it over there," Jill was

assuring her. "And they're all crazy to meet you."

As, just a few short weeks ago, Holly would have been 'crazy' to meet them.

"And if you're worried about that boyfriend of yours," said Jill, who'd never really taken to Brian, "don't be! You deserve a change."

Mercifully, the next ten days gave Holly no time to think. Leaving her flat ready for its next occupant, and the office free of problems, took up every minute of the day and much of the night. Ringing the Book Shop on the night before she was due to fly out to join Jill in New York she was relieved and yet, at the same time, bitterly disappointed — to hear Mike answer. Everyone else, apparently was out, and he only just happened to be there waiting for Abbie to come back when the telephone rang.

Yes, he told her, everything was fine and the bakery was doing well now that the Baxters were back, and they had Sir Henry's regular order. They were even contemplating building a second oven. And yes, he'd tell everyone she'd rung and he, personally, would like to wish her the very best of luck in her new life.

When she'd rung off Holly sat for several minutes, staring into space. She was naturally pleased that the bakery was now such a flourishing concern, but it still hurt a little that they were obviously managing so well without her. It would have soothed her pride to have been missed — just a little. She felt the tears begin to prickle and put up an impatient hand to dash them away. There was still too much to be done to give way to the luxury of tears. And perhaps, after all, someone might ring back when they heard from Mike about her journey to the States, if only to wish her luck.

But no call came that night, or in the morning before Brian picked her up to drive her to the airport. The sooner she left England the better, she thought, as they walked from the car-park to the terminal building. But they walked through fog, and she wasn't surprised when her flight was delayed until visibility had improved.

"Coffee?" Brian suggested.

"There's no need for you to wait," she told him. "I know you're busy."

He looked pleased to be reminded of it. "Rushed off my feet, as a matter of fact. But I can still spare a few minutes."

It was strange, she was to think later, how those few minutes were to change the course of her whole life.

With the coffee Brian brought a couple of currant buns. "Don't expect they'll be as good as Marlingham buns! By the way, have you heard how they're managing without you?"

"Very well!" And she told him about the possibility of building a second oven.

"I said at the beginning that it had a great future," he said.

Since this was precisely what he had *not* said at the beginning, Holly found it difficult not to smile.

"And Lorimer?" Brian pursued. "I suppose, now that you're off to the

States and Olivia Harding's marrying Sir Henry, he'll be looking for a new girlfriend."

Holly almost dropped her coffee-cup. "*What* did you say?"

"He'll be looking for a new girlfriend. You can't blame him for that, surely?"

"No — before that. Olivia Harding is marrying . . . ?"

"Sir Henry Jarvis. D'you mean to say you didn't know?"

Incapable of coherent speech, Holly could only shake her head.

"I would have thought you'd have been one of the first to know. And anyway, it was in all the papers the other day. Millionaire magnate to marry beautiful art connoisseur."

"I haven't had time to look at the papers," said Holly.

"With his money and her taste, their house will be a showpiece. Or houses, I should say! There's a villa in the south of France, a chalet in Switzerland, a . . . where are you off to? Your flight hasn't been called."

"To cancel my flight and then send a cable," said Holly. "Jill said I could take as long as I needed."

"And then where are you going?" asked the bemused Brian.

"Marlingham!" said Holly. "And I'd be more than grateful if you could run me to Euston in your car."

It was almost dusk when she paid off her taxi and started to walk up Bun Lane towards Rosemary Cottage, black against the pink and gold of a dramatic sunset. Both bakery and cottage were in darkness, but soon, she knew, someone would be coming up the lane to get ready for the morning. And it could be John. And then she remembered that the Baxters were back at work now. It was far more likely to be Bill Baxter.

She let herself into the cottage, put her suitcase in the hall, and then wandered slowly about, switching on lights and leaving them burning while she renewed acquaintance with each familiar room. The living-room where John's lamp still stood in the window and someone, she was pleased to see, had been watering the cyclamen; the kitchen, where everything was far too neat and tidy for her liking, and she took mugs out of the cupboard, filled the kettle and put it over a low heat. Then, up the narrow staircase to the landing and her bedroom where the honeycomb quilt Caroline had given her lay smoothly over the divan and the little kidney-shaped dressing-table still waited for the frilly curtains to hide her cosmetic jars. Into the bathroom, the walls freshly painted a delicate eggshell blue but still needing that one, newly plastered wall behind the minuscule bath to be papered; after the style of an English woodland, John had suggested. 'I've seen just the paper. Tree-trunks and rabbits, primroses on a mossy bank. I'll buy a couple of rolls next time I'm in Aylesbury.' But the purchase had never been made.

From the window of the spare bedroom where Abbie had spent the occasional night on a camp-bed Holly looked down

Bun Lane and saw that someone was walking quickly up it. In the now almost total darkness it was impossible to tell who it was. Slowly she went downstairs. Whoever it was they could hardly have failed to notice that the cottage was now lit from stem to stern. And the front door open.

She went through into the kitchen, and stood with her back to the door, busying herself with tea-bags and the now steaming kettle. The knocker fell twice on the front door, and she called in a shaky voice, "Come in!" and heard footsteps crossing the sitting-room and pause behind her.

"Hello, Holly!" said John Lorimer.

She turned and looked at him. All the way down in the train she had rehearsed what she would say when this moment came. Impossible to blurt out, 'I thought you were going to marry Olivia!' So it would have to be some ridiculous, inconsequential remark like 'Couldn't go without wishing you a happy Christmas!' or 'Found I'd left my favourite tooth-brush behind!'

But now they were actually standing face to face and she saw the wonderment in his face all she could say in a funny, choked voice was, "I've come back!"

"Thank God that you have!" he said, and held out his arms. Like a bird to its nest, she went into them.

At first he simply held her fast as if he would never let her go. And then he put a finger under her chin and tilted it back so that he could look down into her eyes. "Home for good?" he asked.

"If you want me!"

"There's no adequate answer to that, beyond saying that I love you, and if you were not going to stay I don't know how I'd manage to get through the rest of my life. You have absolutely no idea how much I've missed you!" And he brought his mouth down hard upon hers.

Several moments later she drew breath. "And I thought you were going to marry Olivia!"

He laughed. "It crossed my mind that you might be thinking that. But then it didn't really seem important what you thought, if you were going to marry Brian. I take it," he raised an eyebrow, "that you're not!"

"Of course not! Although if it hadn't been for him telling me that Olivia was going to marry Sir Henry I wouldn't be here now."

"Then I owe him a great deal," he said. "And I never thought I'd hear myself saying that!"

"There is one thing I should tell you straight away," said Holly. "I may have to go to the States for a while. Just until Jill can find someone else to take my place."

"Mike told us at lunch-time today that you were going, so I've had a few hours to get used to the idea. But then, of course, I thought you were never coming back! By the way, is that a pot of tea on the table? Lets have a cup while we sort out a few details. Not that anything else really matters except that you're home again."

While Holly poured the tea he put a

match to the kindling in the inglenook and threw on an armful of logs. At first, they sat on either side of it, feeding the flames and drinking their tea, but then, because this entailed an unbearable distance between them, Holly went and curled up on the rug at his feet.

"Aren't you supposed to be getting the bakery ready for the morning?"

"No, that's Bill Baxter's job now, I'm pleased to say."

"Then what brought you up Bun Lane at this time of day?"

He kissed the top of her head. "You wouldn't know this, but it's possible, if you happen to be in one of the attics where I keep my stock, to see the roof and first-floor windows of Rosemary Cottage. I was up there about half an hour ago and noticed the place was ablaze with light and thought I should come and investigate. It seemed too much to hope," his lips brushed her hair again, "that I should find you here."

She looked up at him and asked the inevitable question. "When did you first know that . . . you loved me?" It was still difficult to say the incredible words.

"Unknown to myself probably from the first moment I saw you standing in the square and looking in through the windows of the shop, but I didn't realise it until I'd kissed you — that first time when I walked you home, and we'd furnished this room for you, without your knowing."

So it had been magic for him, too! The realisation made it imperative that she kiss him again — a difficult task from where she was sitting. John bent and scooped her up in his arms, and together they made the delightful discovery that one chair was quite big enough for two. Some time later Holly picked up the threads of her enquiry.

"What I still don't understand is why — if you felt like that — you should have suddenly treated me so coolly!"

"Because, my dear child, I thought you were in love with Brian and were just showing your gratitude towards me.

I couldn't honestly see how marriage to Brian was going to work out for you, but if that was the way you wanted it that was the way it had to be. And another thing — I was convinced I would be too old for you anyway."

"Don't be so ridiculous!"

Showing him just how ridiculous took several minutes more.

"And then, of course," she continued dreamily, "I was so sure you were in love with Olivia."

"*Now*, who's being ridiculous? Although I am very fond of her — in a brotherly sort of way. But I'm not at all sure that Olivia is capable of falling deeply in love, as I know that you and I are."

"You mean, she doesn't love Sir Henry?"

"Oh, they're both very fond of each other, and I'm certain that they're going to be perfectly happy together. For the first time in her life Olivia will be able to indulge her craving for beautiful things and be able to keep them for herself instead of selling them to other people. She'll spend his money with the best possible taste and always look exquisitely groomed, and he'll be very proud of her."

"That's more or less what Brian said when he told me they were engaged."

"If you hadn't left here in such a hurry you would have found out when everyone else did! They announced it the day after you left."

"And the bakery?" She was slowly working through her mental list of questions. "That's all right now?"

"Making a very nice turnover, I'm pleased to report. Thanks to Sir Henry and Brian."

"Incidentally," she said, "did you realise that Brian spoke to Sir Henry entirely of his own accord? I certainly didn't suggest it to him."

"Yes, when I eventually saw Sir Henry I knew from the timing of their meeting that it couldn't have been your idea. You and I were jogging home behind Daisy Belle when they were discussing it. But at the time I must admit I thought you'd taken matters into your own hands without consulting me. I wouldn't have blamed you, either! I hadn't exactly made a success of things."

"We would have survived," she told him confidently.

"Probably. But only just. As it is, we've gone from strength to strength. By the way, when do you have to be in the States?"

She explained that Jill had said she was to stay in England as long as it was necessary — and didn't John agree that this came under the heading of 'necessary'?

"Absolutely vital!" he assured her.

"But I mustn't stay too long, although I shall hate leaving you now, even for a few weeks."

"My publisher," he said thoughtfully, "was saying the other day that a personal appearance over there might make a big difference to the sales of my book."

"You mean you could come with me? Oh, John!"

"And you're sure that you won't mind

marrying a book-seller-cum-scribbler?"

"Cum-baker!" she reminded him, nestling into his arms.

THE END

WITH SOMEBODY ELSE
Theresa Charles

Rosamond sets off for Cornwall with Hugo to meet his family, blissfully unaware of the shocks in store for her.

A SUMMER FOR STRANGERS
Claire Hamilton

Because she had lost her job, her flat and she had no money, Tabitha agreed to pose as Adam's future wife although she believed the scheme to be deceitful and cruel.

VILLA OF SINGING WATER
Angela Petron

The disquieting incidents that occurred at the Vatican and the Colosseum did not trouble Jan at first, but then they became increasingly unpleasant and alarming.

DOCTOR NAPIER'S NURSE
Pauline Ash

When cousins Midge and Derry are entered as probationer nurses on the same day but at different hospitals they agree to exchange identities.

A GIRL LIKE JULIE
Louise Ellis

Caroline absolutely adored Hugh Barrington, but then Julie Crane came into their lives. Julie was the kind of girl who attracts men without even trying.

COUNTRY DOCTOR
Paula Lindsay

When Evan Richmond bought a practice in a remote country village he did not realise that a casual encounter would lead to the loss of his heart.

ENCORE
Helga Moray

Craig and Janet realise that their true happiness lies with each other, but it is only under traumatic circumstances that they can be reunited.

NICOLETTE
Ivy Preston

When Grant Alston came back into her life, Nicolette was faced with a dilemma. Should she follow the path of duty or the path of love?

THE GOLDEN PUMA
Margaret Way

Catherine's time was spent looking after her father's Queensland farm. But what life was there without David, who wasn't interested in her?